82

SUSAN FLETCHER

SHADOW SPINNER

A JEAN KARL BOOK

ALADDIN PAPERBACKS

First Aladdin Paperbacks edition November 1999

Copyright © 1998 by Susan Fletcher

Aladdin Paperbacks
An imprint of Simon & Schuster
Children's Publishing Division
1230 Avenue of the Americas
New York, NY 10020

Also available in an Atheneum Books for Young Readers hardcover edition.
Book design by Angela Carlino
The text for this book was set in Adobe Caslon.
Manufactured in the United States of America
20 19

The Library of Congress has cataloged the hardcover edition as follows:
Fletcher, Susan, 1951–
Shadow Spinner / by Susan Fletcher.
p. cm.
"A Jean Karl book."
Summary: When Marjan, a thirteen-year-old crippled girl, joins the
Sultan's harem in ancient Persia, she gathers for Shahrazad the stories
which will save the queen's life.
ISBN-13: 978-0-689-81852-3 ISBN-10: 0-689-81852-1 (hc.)
1. Scheherazade (Legendary character)—Juvenile fiction. [1. Scheherazade
(Legendary character)—Fiction. 2. Storytellers—Fiction. 3. Physically handicapped—
Fiction. 4. Interpersonal relations—Fiction. 5. Iran—Fiction.] I. Title.
PZ7.F6356Sh 1998
[Fic]—dc21 97-37346 CIP AC
ISBN-13: 978-0-689-83051-8 (pbk.)
ISBN-10: 0-689-83051-3 (pbk.)

*For Jean Karl, who has taught
me so much about story*

I could not have written this book without the generous help of many people! Dr. Abbas Milani read the manuscript twice—once by candlelight during a power outage. Besides catching my mistakes and answering multiple queries, he made many suggestions that greatly enhanced the book. Zohré Bullock graciously regaled me with tea, coffee, and cookies while answering my interminable questions. I am also very much indebted to the wisdom of Dr. John Stewart, Sue Chism, Will Earhart, Eric Kimmel, Susan Ash, Jackie Rose, Eloise and Bill McGraw, the members of my two critique groups, Susan Strauss, Becky Huntting, and, of course, Jean Karl.

Chapter 1
Within the Harem Doors

My auntie Chava used to say to me, "What's going to be*come* of you, Marjan?" She would usually say this when I had done something foolish—tipped over the olive jar, maybe, or daydreamed over the coals until the lentils were burnt. But I knew she meant it in another way, too, because I would probably never marry. No one would want a bride with one foot maimed and turned askew. Even though I could run fast and carry a pot on my head and cook a lamb stew as well as other girls, my foot would be seen as bad luck. An ill omen. So all my life I would have to live on the charity of my relatives—except that I had no relatives anymore. Auntie Chava was not my real aunt, and she and Uncle Eli were old and had fallen on hard times. No one would have any use for me when they were gone.

So Auntie Chava would cast up her gaze and sigh and ask, "What's going to be*come* of you, Marjan?"

You can never really know what's going to happen to a person in this life. What actually became of *me*, no one would have guessed.

The first time I set foot inside the Sultan's harem, I was hoping to catch a glimpse of Shahrazad.

Shahrazad was my hero. She had offered to marry the Sultan when he was killing all his wives. Marry one at night, kill her the next morning—that's what he did.

Until Shahrazad.

"Keep your eyes downcast, Marjan, and make sure your hair is covered," Auntie Chava warned me as we passed through the gates to the palace and crossed the outer courtyard. "There are women in there in all manner of dress and undress—but here you keep your modesty."

I clutched my long veil, holding it snug beneath my chin so that only the moon of my face would show. The sun glared blindingly on the marble floor and glittered in the fountain. I looked for the harem door, but the shadows that shrouded the far side of the courtyard were blue-black and opaque.

Though I was eager to see the harem, I was a little bit scared, too. I had heard the tales of fountains running red with blood after the Sultan discovered his first wife with another man. He had slain her and all of her servants and slaves—every grown woman in the harem, save for his own mother. The Sultan vowed then and there that no woman would ever betray him again. That's why he started killing off his wives.

Auntie Chava stopped now in the shadows before a pair of high wooden doors. She spoke to the guards. They looked stern in their high helmets, with daggers and gleaming scimitars hanging from their belts. It had been many years since Auntie Chava had come here—not since Uncle Eli had lost his fortune when a merchant ship went down. Before that, she used to come often to the

2

harem, selling jewels and silks from distant lands. But now, though I had begged her to let me come, I was having second thoughts. *Third* thoughts, when the doors groaned and boomed heavily behind, shutting us into a dim hallway with two barefoot harem eunuchs. *Once a woman enters those gates, she never comes out alive,* was what they said of the Sultan's harem. And mostly, that was true.

Still, we had come only to sell things to the harem women, so they *would* let us out. For certain, Auntie Chava had assured me.

I could not see well at first, for my eyes had not yet adjusted to the sudden darkness. Walking carefully to hide my limp, I followed the shape of Auntie Chava's floor-length veil as she followed one of the eunuchs. Cool air washed over me—a relief from the heat of the sun. Soon, I heard a plash of water and smelled a delicious intermingling of flowers and sandalwood and cloves. By the time I could well make out my surroundings, we had passed through another gate and into a courtyard.

It was not an open court, though it seemed so. The domed roof looked almost as high as the sky. Honeyed light sifted in through carved wooden screens, gilding the walls and floors. Light danced in the spray of a fountain, shimmered like liquid silver on the surface of the pool. Birds flitted among fruit trees and blossoming bushes, which filled the air with their sweet smells. The floors were inlaid with jewel-bright tiles and spread with fine woolen carpets embroidered in crimson and gold.

I looked for the rusty tinge of bloodstains on the fountain's tiles but, save for their colored borders, they were white as a turnip's flesh.

The eunuch settled himself upon a cushion in a corner;

I sneaked a furtive peak at him. He was dark-skinned and, except for his fine silk robes, looked much as other eunuchs I had seen—smooth-faced and heavy about the hips.

Auntie Chava shed her veil, then opened her bundle, spread out the cloth, and began arranging her wares on it. They were her very own treasures from the time when she had been wealthy: jeweled rings and bracelets and neck chains, lengths of satin and damask and silk. Uncle Eli had not wanted her to sell them but, "We must pay the taxes," Auntie Chava said. I looked at her now, to see if she seemed sorry to let her things go. She set them out briskly. But I saw her hands linger for a moment on a brooch of lapis lazuli before she laid it gently down.

The room was silent, save for the splash and gurgle of the fountain. But soon, as if we had set off some unheard signal, there came the pattering of bare feet on tile. There was a whispering of voices, a jingling of bracelets, a rustling of cloth.

I could picture her then—Shahrazad—slim and regal, moving gracefully across the court as if she held an invisible water jar balanced upon her head. She would not be overeager; not greedy. She would greet Auntie Chava and then turn to me, and something in my eyes would hold her. Would she sense that I, too, made an art of telling old tales? Would she know, somehow, that *she* was my inspiration? That I wanted to be just like her?

"Marjan! Get your mind out of the mist and put out your wares!"

Hastily, I took off my veil, untied my bundle, and set out Auntie Chava's jewels and ribbons and silks. I heard her muttering under her breath, "What's going to be*come* of you, Marjan?"

4

And then here they came, the harem women, gliding through the archways into the courtyard—their bright-hued gowns fluttering, their voices softly chattering—for all the world like a flight of beautiful birds. They gathered around us, enveloped us in a thick, sweet cloud of perfume—trying on bracelets and rings, remarking upon the color of a stone, the sheen of a length of silk. The jewels caught the light and cast it in dizzying flecks across the floor and walls. Though none of the women were as naked as Auntie Chava would have had me believe, many wore alluring garments that revealed bare arms and throats and the curved shapes of breasts and hips.

I searched their faces for Shahrazad, for I felt, though I had never seen her, that I would *know* her. Many of these women would be relatives of the Sultan—distant aunts or nieces who had been widowed or divorced by their husbands and had nowhere else to go. Because they were not virgins, the formerly married relatives were in no danger of being wedded to the Sultan. Other harem women were slaves—though few were young and beautiful, as harem slaves usually are. Before he married Shahrazad, the Sultan had used up all the young and beautiful virgins as wives.

Still, I noticed five or six young women—new, no doubt, since Shahrazad had stopped the killings. They were dazzling, the young women. But they came too fast and eager, snatching at Auntie Chava's treasures. None was Shahrazad, I felt certain.

I answered their questions, telling how this length of satin came from Samarkand, how that bracelet was of hammered Indian copper. Soon everything was taken; there was nothing for me to do but gather up our bundle cloths and wait. Auntie Chava would do the bargaining. It would take time, I knew.

It was then, while I was kneeling to fold the cloths, that I saw the children. They must have come in behind the women, and I had been so caught up in the fever of trade that I hadn't noticed. But now they drew slowly near, staring at me with bold curiosity. There were a dozen or so of them, ranging, I guessed, from three to eight years old. Harem children. Some belonged to the harem women; others were orphans of distant relations of the Sultan; still others were children or grandchildren of favored slaves.

I worried about the girls.

A pet gazelle trotted up behind one of the children—she was six or seven years old, I guessed. The gazelle nudged her hand; she scratched behind its ears, not moving her gaze from me.

"What's wrong with your foot?" the gazelle girl asked.

I sat back on my heels and briskly pulled my gown to cover my crippled foot.

"What's *wrong* with it? It looks strange."

"Nothing," I said shortly.

One little boy crept forward, shyly reaching out to touch my sleeve, then pulled quickly back. He held his nose and pointed at me. The other children giggled, but neither backed away nor unfastened their gazes from my face.

Likely they had never seen a girl *not* decked out in silk and damask, *not* bathed and scrubbed raw, *not* brushed and perfumed until she gleamed and reeked of flowers. They looked at me as if I were some outlandish creature. I might as well have been an Abyssinian, or a jinn. Yet to me, they were likewise strange.

Wondrous strange.

Slowly, I stretched out my hand to touch the silken sleeve of the boy who had touched mine. But he jerked back, and they all moved, in a flock, away. I wished I had some sweets to tempt them to eat out of my hand, like the sparrows that nested in the pomegranate tree in Uncle Eli's courtyard.

But I had other lures.

I glanced at Auntie Chava, still deep in money dealings with the harem women. This could take forever.

"Have you heard," I asked the children, "the tale of the fisherman and the jinn?"

Several solemn heads shook *no*, but the girl with the gazelle piped up, "I have! The jinn was going to kill him, but the fisherman tricked it."

"Yes," I said, "but did you know about the talking fish?"

She narrowed her eyes warily, shook her head.

"Well, the jinn told the fisherman to cast his net again. And it came up with four fishes in it: one white, one red, one blue, one yellow."

"There's no such thing as a blue fish," the girl said.

"Well yes there is because this one was. Only, they were magical fishes. Because when the fisherman sold them to the Sultan, and the Sultan gave them to his cook, and the cook began to fry them, the wall cracked open with a *boom!* And a beautiful lady came in through the crack. And then the fishes lifted up their heads and talked to her."

I held my breath then, waiting. It is not good, when telling tales, to tell too much too soon. You must cast your net, like the fisherman in the story, then wait to see what swims in.

The children watched me, eyes wide. At last, just when I feared that I would lose them, the gazelle girl said, "What did the fish . . . *say?*"

And then I knew I had them.

I spun the old tale carefully, meting out mystery upon mystery and not solving one until after the next had been posed. I spoke softly, then loudly, then softly again, so that the children crept ever nearer. Soon they were ringed all about me, touching me. I breathed in their sweet perfume. One little girl laid her head on my knee and looked straight up into my face. A boy clutched the hem of my gown as he sucked his thumb. The gazelle folded its long legs and nuzzled at my hands. And the tale took on a life of its own, as tales sometimes do, enfolding me in the world of it, opening up to show me particulars I had never seen before in all the times I had told it.

"And the sorceress lost no time, but betook herself to the shores of that lake, where she sprinkled the waters on the sand. And she spoke some words over the fish—*balanka balinka baloo!* And the fishes jumped up and turned into men and women and children! One of them had hair that curled just like yours," I said to the gazelle girl, "and was wearing a silver bracelet like this one, and a gown of blue silk just like the one you're wearing . . ." I stopped, furrowed my brow at her. "Are you *certain* you've never been a fish?"

A muffled laugh sounded from outside the circle of children; I looked up sharply. My eyes met the gaze of a girl a little older than me—fourteen or fifteen, I guessed. She was dressed more simply than the women, but I knew by the drape and sheen of her yellow silk gown that the fabric was exceedingly fine. Her eyes, clear gray and almond-shaped, were serious, even before the dimpled smile faded from her mouth.

"Go on," she said. "Please."

It was a request—not a demand—and yet I could tell by some quality of her voice that she was accustomed to being obliged.

Who *was* she?

I darted a look at where the other women were still bargaining with Auntie Chava. They showed no deference to this girl, nor even seemed to notice her.

Flustered, I did go on, but I was out of the tale now, fixed firmly in the *now* of the harem. I finished quickly; the children begged for more.

"Not now, little ones," the gray-eyed girl said. "Go and play!"

They scattered like a covey of partridges and disappeared through an arched doorway, trailing echoes of talk and laughter. The gazelle hesitated, then bounded after.

Now the gray-eyed girl drew near; hastily, I clambered to my feet. She was not tall, I saw, barely taller than I. Her face was lovely—square-jawed, with a full, wide mouth and plump cheeks that dimpled when she smiled. Her hair, a thick, glossy braid, lay draped over her shoulder. But she seemed unaware of her beauty. There was no smugness about this girl, no fluttering. "Do you know other tales?" she asked.

I nodded, not trusting my voice. I knew many old tales; I collected them. I had trained myself to fix a tale in memory, so I would never forget. But . . . who *was* this girl?

"Wait here," she said.

I stood awkwardly, watching as the girl spoke with Auntie Chava and then with another of the older women.

Suddenly, I wanted to go to Auntie Chava, to have her put her arm around me, to leave this place and go home. But the girl had said, *Wait here.*

Auntie Chava glanced at me and said something to the girl. Their voices were soft; I couldn't hear. Then the girl came back.

"Come with me," she said.

I stood rooted. I looked beseechingly back at Auntie Chava, who nodded as if to reassure me.

"Come," the girl said.

I looked again at Auntie Chava; she made a shooing motion with her hand.

The girl hastened across the courtyard and disappeared through an archway. I had to move fast to catch up, struggling to hide my limp. Auntie Chava wouldn't have . . . *sold* me, would she? Fear rose up within me. *Once a woman enters these gates, she never comes out alive.*

"Where are we going?" I said to the girl's back.

The girl didn't slow a bit. She had a powerful stride. Though Auntie Chava said that harem women lounged on cushions all day drinking sharbats, I doubted *this* one did.

"Where are we *going*?" I asked again, louder.

"To see my sister," the girl said over her shoulder.

"Your . . . sister?"

"Yes! My sister . . . Shahrazad."

Chapter 2
Shahrazad

LESSONS FOR LIFE AND STORYTELLING

My auntie Chava always said I was an impractical child. "Keep your mind out of the mist, Marjan!" she was always telling me. "Be practical—look to your own survival!" She did not approve of my telling old tales to the neighborhood children (though I often caught her listening in). "Spinning shadows," she would call it, then she would sniff her most disdainful sniff.

But I would say to her, "Look at Shahrazad. Telling stories can be *very* practical.

"Stories can save your life."

Of course I knew that Shahrazad had a sister. Everyone knew that. On the night she married the Sultan, Shahrazad had asked if she could tell one last story to her younger sister before dawn, before he killed Shahrazad. The Sultan said yes, and so, a little while before dawn, they sent for the sister. The Sultan listened as Shahrazad told the story. When Shahrazad saw that daybreak was approaching, she broke off her story in the middle of an exciting part, and the Sultan let her live until the next night so he could hear how things turned out.

But on the second night, the same thing happened: they sent for her sister, Shahrazad left off spinning her story at another exciting part, and the Sultan let her live again.

And it had gone on that way for more than two and a half years. During that time, Shahrazad had given the Sultan three sons—one just this past week. Now everyone in the city breathed easier. People no longer hid their daughters or sent them away with Abu Muslem, the famous outlaw who helped women escape. Shahrazad had stopped the killings.

So I *had* heard of Dunyazad, Shahrazad's sister. But somehow I had never thought about her very much.

Until now.

The main thing I kept thinking about her now was, *I wish that she'd slow down.* She kept disappearing behind screens and walls and archways, and I had to run to keep from losing her. She skirted a deserted open courtyard where ruby-throated birds perched in fragrant trees, then she crossed a stream that gurgled between banks of vivid blue tile. She opened a hidden paneled door and climbed into a dim, musty-smelling passageway that wound this way and that. Through tiny windows I could glimpse other empty rooms and courtyards, each decorated with tilework and carvings and gold. We came out at a marble colonnade near a wide flight of green-glazed steps; Dunyazad bounded up, then strode across a high balcony that overlooked a courtyard below. Reaching into a cranny of a carved wooden screen, she released a hidden latch, opened it, then plunged down the narrow stairway beyond.

And all the while I saw not a single living soul. There was a hushed, eerie feeling to this place. All those sofas with no one to sit on them. All that beauty with no one to see. Beyond the echoes of our footsteps, I could almost hear the whispered voices of the women who had lived here before the Sultan's purge.

All gone now. All slain.

I followed Dunyazad down the stairs to a hallway floored in gray marble. She ducked into a small draped cubicle and seemed to have vanished entirely until I heard a rattling sound and pulled the drape aside. Through a beaded curtain, I glimpsed a ripple of yellow silk; I hastened after it into a courtyard.

My foot was hurting now; it does when I go far or fast. But worse than the pain was the mounting fear that I would be lost. I could wander through this labyrinth and not find my way out for days. Weeks, maybe. I would have to drink the water in the pools. I would have to catch the fish that darted within them, eat them raw. Or maybe they would lift up their heads and talk to me, tell me how . . .

Stop spinning shadows! I told myself sternly. *Look to your own survival!*

"Here." Dunyazad was climbing a flight of stairs to a high-arched doorway off an alabaster-tiled corridor. She disappeared within; I heard a voice, a greeting.

Shahrazad?

And now I stopped, uncertain.

I looked down at my coarse gown—at its faded brown color, at the stains that would not come out no matter how hard I scrubbed, at the fresh rime of dust from dragging through the streets. And I felt . . . ashamed to appear before Shahrazad. I brushed at the dust, but it was no use.

From the shadowed hallway where I stood, I could see only a narrow strip of one wall of the room beyond the

13

arch. Sunlight streamed in through a high mosaic of colored glass and through a carved wooden screen below.

Dunyazad reappeared in the arch. "Come! She awaits!"

Slowly, I edged through the arch . . .

And nearly tripped over a stack of books.

Books! They were everywhere—strewn all over the sofas, all over the carpeted floor. Stacks and drifts and mounds of them—some open, some shut. And scrolls! They were littered all about the books. A fortune in books and scrolls.

And there, kneeling on the floor, one finger poised upon the page of an open book . . . was Shahrazad.

I *did* know her at once, though I don't know exactly how. She was not at all the way I had imagined her. True, she was beautiful, even though she wore a robe from the baths and her long hair hung wet and uncombed down her back. Her skin was clear and glowing, her lips full, her eyebrows pleasingly arched, her lashes a thick, dark fringe. But what shocked me was her eyes. Haunted, hunted eyes. There was a look in them that dwelt somewhere in the spaces between hunger and terror.

I had seen that look before in the eyes of a thief condemned to death. But here, in the eyes of the hero of my life, it chilled me to the bone.

I moved forward, knelt, and kissed the floor before her.

"Tell her that story about the fish—the one you were telling the children," Dunyazad said.

I swallowed. *I?* Tell a story to Shahrazad? But she was the one who had inspired *me* to tell stories. I only told stories because of her.

"*Tell* her," Dunyazad insisted.

I swallowed again, licked my lips. "A jinn told a fisherman to . . . to cast his net . . . into the sea," I began haltingly.

Shahrazad moved her hand from the page. She fixed her haunted gaze upon my face. It was difficult, with her staring so, to latch on to the tale. "The net came up with four fish in it—one white, one red, one blue, one yellow," I said. "But when the fisherman sold them to the Sultan . . ." It was coming now, though in starts and lurches. As I went on, Shahrazad leaned toward me, seemed to devour me with her eyes. "And lifting up his robe, he showed the Sultan that he was a man only from his head to his waist, and that his feet and legs and hips were made of black marble—"

"No!"

The voice came harsh and sudden; I broke off the tale and gaped.

Shahrazad turned to her sister. "I told this story long ago. Don't you remember? It was one of the early ones."

Dunyazad sighed. "It did sound more familiar this second time. But . . ." She turned to me. "Tell her another tale. You said you know others."

I *did* know other tales, but they all fled my mind in the heat of Shahrazad's gaze. Fragments of stories I knew racketed about my mind—a magic lamp, a wealthy portress, a foolish weaver. I seized upon this last and began, haltingly followed the thread of the tale. But just when it was coming clear to me, Shahrazad cried, "No! I've told it!"

I tried tale after tale, dragging each one up through the tumult in my mind until I could find the shape of it. But each time Shahrazad broke in before I was well

15

along. Most of them she had told the Sultan before; a few she thought he wouldn't like. "He yawned when I told a story very like that one," she said. "*Yawned!* I *musn't* tell tales that make him yawn!" And once she said something odd—something I would have questioned her about if I had dared: "He's not ready for that one yet," she said.

I went through all my stock of old tales, the ones I tell the neighborhood children. They're not so choosy as the Sultan. They love hearing their favorites over and over. At last I remembered a tale I had heard one day from a story-teller in the bazaar—a tale of a mermaid named Julnar.

"So she swam out of the sea and rested on the shore of an island under the full moon, and a man who was passing by found her. He took her home and tried to make love to her, but she hit him on the head. So he sold her to a merchant . . ."

Shahrazad moved toward me until her face was so close that I could have counted her eyelashes. The sweet musk of her perfume filled my nose. Her eyes never left mine; I was pinioned in her gaze. She grasped my wrist hard—until it hurt—but I dared not protest. "I've not heard this before," she whispered. "I've not heard this."

When at last I came to the end of the tale, Shahrazad let out a deep sigh. She unclasped my wrist, stared dazedly down at the white finger marks on my skin.

"What is your name?" she asked, looking up at last.

"Marjan," I said.

"Marjan." She spoke my name as if tasting it, as if it were some rare delicacy served for the very first time. She breathed deeply; some of the tautness drained from her face. "Well, Marjan," she said. "You have told me a tale that I have never heard before. And that is quite a feat, for I know many tales. And that is also *good*, for the Sultan does not fancy a tale twice-told. His memory is sharp. I lose track of them, there have been so many . . . He complains when the tales seem too much alike."

"We should have written down which tales she's told, from the very start," Dunyazad said. "We think she might know some she *hasn't* told, or she could find some in her books. But they're all starting to sound alike. It's hard to be certain. We *need* to be certain."

"Couldn't you . . . make up some stories?" I asked.

Though I mostly told old tales, sometimes they veered off in strange new directions while I was telling them. I tried not to do this, because I wanted to be just like Shahrazad, and I had heard that she stayed faithful to the old tales. Other times, when I was daydreaming, I invented stories that were completely new. But I hardly ever *told* them—except when I ran out of old stories to tell.

"I have made up a few," Shahrazad said, "though it's hard. I always like the old tales better than anything I can think up. And I can't seem to make up anything new right now. They all begin to sound familiar, and I'm afraid I'm just *remembering*—not inventing."

"Being so tired doesn't help," Dunyazad said. "She just gave birth five days ago."

I nodded. Everybody knew. Criers had run through the streets announcing it, and everywhere people had celebrated.

"I never thought . . ." Shahrazad shook her head. "I knew it would take time for the stories to do their work, but . . . Nine hundred eighty-nine nights it's been! *Nine hundred eighty-nine nights!*"

Slowly, she rose to her feet, began to pace back and forth in an uncluttered patch of carpet. She was tall, I saw. Long and slender of neck and arm and leg. Much taller than her younger sister. Her movements were not lively, like Dunyazad's, but graceful. Like a swan. And it seemed to me that some power was beginning to fill her—some power that had been drained before.

"This king," she said. "What did you say his name was?"

"Shahriman," I said.

"Shahriman." Shahrazad stopped for a moment, closing her eyes. "Shahriman." She opened her eyes and began once again to pace. "So King Shahriman owned a hundred concubines but none of them had given him a child. One day as he was lamenting this, one of his guards came to him and said, 'My lord, at the door is a merchant with a slave girl who is more beautiful than the moon.' Do I have it so far, Marjan?"

"Yes," I said.

"And she was as beautiful as the merchant had said. But when the king asked her name, she did not say a word. Only her beauty protected her from his anger. And then he asked . . . Who was it he asked, Marjan? The merchant? Or his guard? Or his slave girls?"

"His slave girls."

"Yes, now I remember. He asked his slave girls whether the girl had spoken, and they said, 'From the time of her coming until now she has not uttered one word.'"

Then Shahrazad told *us* Julnar's story, stopping, from time to time, to ask about this detail or that. She told how at last, when Julnar was with child, she spoke to Shahriman about herself, how she was the daughter of the King

18

of the High Seas, how her father had died and his kingdom had been seized. Julnar had quarreled with her brother and had thrown herself upon the mercy of a man from the land, who had sold her to the merchant, who had sold her to Shahriman. Then Shahrazad told how Julnar begged the king to let her summon her family for the birthing, because women of the land do not know how women of the sea give birth to children. "Let me know when I go astray, Marjan," Shahrazad said. "I want to learn it exactly as you told it."

So intent was I upon teaching the tale that I did not see the three women standing outside the archway until Dunyazad motioned them impatiently to come in. They advanced upon us, arms laden with gowns and robes, jewelry and jars, brushes and vials. They surrounded Shahrazad. One woman whisked off the queen's robe and began dressing her in layer upon layer of silks. Another began combing her hair; the third daubed and brushed at her face, filling the air with a fog of fragrant powder.

And all the while Shahrazad practiced, telling the tale over and over, making some parts fast and others slow, making some parts loud and others soft—binding them all together in a pleasing cadence, like a song. When she spoke of the ocean, you could almost hear the boom and hiss of it in her voice. When she told about Julnar, she seemed to slip inside the skin of a sea creature and move in a watery way. Soon, she stopped asking me questions and posed them to herself. "Shall I stop here, tonight," she wondered, "or later in the tale? Shall I word it thisly, or thusly?"

In time, the story came unbroken, as if she had known it all her life.

A slave girl entered, went round lighting the lamps; only then did I realize that it was growing dark. Long, flickering shadows stretched across the room. Shahrazad stood murmuring in a pool of golden lamplight while the women tended to her. A robe of midnight blue hung down over her shoulders. It was purfled with pearls, like stars. Her face looked rapt, serene. It was luminous as the moon.

"Then Julnar kindled a flame in a chafing dish, and she took lign aloes and tossed them into the fire. She spoke some magical words, and all at once a great smoke arose, and the sea began to froth and foam. Presently, Julnar's family arose from the waves: first her brother, Salih, then her mother, Farahshah. They walked across the face of the water until they drew near Julnar's window and recognized her."

And a huge eunuch was standing at the door. He wore a headdress encrusted with jewels, and robes of gleaming cloth-of-gold. His face—black and smooth and hairless—looked distant. Cold. "It is time," he said.

Dunyazad clasped her sister in her arms. When she moved away, I caught the gleam of unshed tears in her eyes. Shahrazad moved toward the eunuch, then paused, walked back to me. She leaned in close, grasped my wrist. "Thank you, Marjan," she whispered. And I saw it then, in her eyes—a quicksilver spasm of fear. But in the next instant, it was gone.

Shahrazad turned, swept out of the room.

I stood beneath the arch and watched for as long as I could as she walked with the eunuch down the alabaster corridor toward the Sultan's bedchamber. Her head was held high, her hips swayed gracefully; she was the picture of serenity. And yet she looked so frail. The lives of all the young women in the harem—all the young women in the city!—rested upon those slender shoulders. Depended upon her ability to please a man who would slay her for a yawn. Hung by the thin thread of a tale I had heard from a beggar in the bazaar. And, now that I had seen the terror behind the mask of Shahrazad's serenity, I only revered her the more.

She was the bravest person I had ever seen in all my entire life.

Chapter 3
The Wish

We were late getting home.

No sooner had we unlocked the gate and stepped into the courtyard than Uncle Eli came hobbling toward us in the twilight, peppering us with questions, his tassels swinging, his yellow turban askew. Where had we been? Were we all right? Why had we taken so long? Had there been trouble? Had we been robbed? He had sent out Old

Mordecai to search for us—or for our dead bodies. They had not known *which* they would find.

"We are fine," Auntie Chava assured him, "and there has been no trouble. Quite the contrary, in fact. We have had . . . a little adventure." She glanced at me, and a smile quirked the corners of her mouth. "Hold out your hands, Eli."

She reached into her sash and took out a handful of coins. A stream of gold dinars clanked into Uncle Eli's knobby, cupped hands. The last few coins slipped off the heap, rang on the tiles. Eli looked up in wonder. "This much?" he said. "But they were not *worth* so much."

"No," Auntie Chava said, "they weren't. It was Marjan who earned the rest of it—with her stories."

Then she told how Dunyazad had taken me to her sister, and how I had told the story, and how Dunyazad had rewarded us with a handful of dinars. Eli funneled the coins into a leather purse; I hunted down the ones on the floor. Then he bade me describe Shahrazad for him—in detail—and tell the mermaid story all over again.

When I had done, Eli tugged at his long white beard, looking pleased. "Don't we have the clever one here, Chava? Didn't I tell you? *Didn't* I?"

It had been Uncle Eli's idea to take me in more than five years before, when I was almost eight. After my mother died, her husband—second husband, not my father—hadn't wanted me in his household anymore, but he couldn't find anyone to take me. Uncle Eli hired me out of pity, I think. Auntie Chava said at the time that I was far too young to be of any use to her; but now, Uncle Eli was always crowing about how smart he had been to discover me.

It's against the law to sell a Muslim as a slave to a Jew,

but Muslims can work for Jews for wages. My mother's husband, Aga Jamsheed, collected several months' wages in advance, and then he and his whole family left the city. Uncle Eli was saving my back wages, just in case Aga Jamsheed ever returned.

Still, Auntie Chava and Uncle Eli didn't treat me as a servant. They treated me as a daughter. He was softer with me than she was. He sneaked me sweets, and he fussed at Auntie Chava not to work me so hard. Sometimes he told me stories from his Scriptures, which reminded me of some of the stories I knew from the Koran.

Now Auntie Chava harrumphed. "Stories won't get dinner cooked," she said.

But they took out the good wine at dinner, and Auntie Chava made me a cup of sharbat. The coins would pay this year's taxes, with some left over for next. When Old Mordecai finally returned, Uncle Eli told him the whole story, exaggerating Dunyazad's praises of me.

"This is an omen," Uncle Eli told Auntie Chava. "Our fortunes are turning—I know it. By this time next year you'll have more jewels and silks than you ever had before. You'll see—I'm right. Those ones you sold today—they're nothing to what you'll have soon."

Auntie Chava smiled—a bit sadly, I thought. "I don't *need* jewels and silks, Eli. I never wear them anyway. This house . . . and you . . . and food enough to keep all of us. *That's* what I want."

It was hard to sleep that night. I kept worrying about Shahrazad. What if the tale I told wasn't good enough? What if it made the Sultan yawn? What if he *hated* it?

I turned it over and over in my mind, noticing how nothing very adventurous actually *happened* in the story, and how the end didn't quite feel right. I fretted about where Shahrazad would break off to make the Sultan want to hear more. There just weren't very many exciting places in that tale. Or none exciting *enough*.

It was a boring tale! I could see that now, though I had not before. It would never save her!

I slept fitfully and woke at dawn. After ablutions and prayers, I got right to work. Busy. I had to keep busy. I milked the goat in darkness, then hauled water from the courtyard well and scrubbed the chipped brown tiles of the floor as the morning sky grew pink. Auntie Chava, I thought, was sleeping *forever* this morning. When finally she awoke, I pestered her to send Old Mordecai to find out if Shahrazad had survived the night. I knew she would never let *me* go out alone.

Auntie Chava admonished me on the virtues of patience, but sent Mordecai for news so promptly that I knew she was worried, too. I hauled more water, started the fire in the brazier, put on a pot of lentils, filled the lamps with oil, mixed dough for a loaf of bread.

Where *was* that Mordecai?

At last, I heard the courtyard door creak open. I froze, afraid, now, to know. Auntie Chava appeared in the archway to her quarters; Uncle Eli came up beside her.

"Well?" Uncle Eli asked.

Old Mordecai smiled his toothless smile and raised his skinny arms high. "She lives."

After that, I danced.

I danced as I polished the lamps. I danced as I refilled the lentil jar. I danced as I sieved the grain, and even as I spun a skein of thread.

It was clumsy dancing, I know, with my bad foot

thunking awkwardly about. But I didn't dance to give others pleasure. I danced for the sheer, giddy joy of it.

"Calm yourself, Marjan!" Auntie Chava kept telling me. "You're going to break something. You're going to hurt yourself. *I'm* going to hurt you—you're making me crazy!"

But I refused to calm myself.

She lives! The most beautiful words I had ever heard!

I spun Julnar's story over and over in my mind, imagining the Sultan's reaction—how he must have laughed at this part or that, how he must have held his breath in suspense, how he must have gasped in wonderment.

It was a splendid tale! I had *always* loved that tale!

I imagined that the Sultan might want more stories like that one. And Shahrazad would send for me. No—not send for me. She would come herself! She and all her retinue: a caravan of silk-turbaned eunuchs and bejeweled serving women. There would be a knock at the gate, and the eunuch would enter—the gold-clad one who had led her to the Sultan. I could see him now, the way he would look, his cloth-of-gold robes shimmering against the dull brown courtyard walls. He would announce Shahrazad, and she would come gliding in, and everyone would kneel and kiss the ground. Then she would touch me on the shoulder and tell me to rise. She would ask me for another tale and, when I had told it, she would open up her purse and out would pour gold coins—enough gold coins to pay all of Uncle Eli and Auntie Chava's taxes . . . forever!

I was so caught up in my daydreams that, after my third spill of oil in the kitchen, Auntie Chava banished me to the back room to mend old clothes.

"And don't prick yourself!" she called after. "Keep your mind on your work!"

And that was why I didn't hear the knock when it came.

The first I knew of it was hearing Auntie Chava's raised voice. I set down my mending, listened. There were other voices, too. Uncle Eli's—sharp, protesting—and another I did not recognize. A man's voice? A woman's? I couldn't tell.

I stood and, throwing on my veil, moved toward the sound of the voices—through the kitchen, into the bright midmorning light of the courtyard, past the well. The voices were coming from Uncle Eli's private rooms. They were quieter now; I couldn't make out what they were saying.

I didn't see the incense burner until I kicked it, sent it clattering across the tiles. The voices stopped. Auntie Chava peered out at me; her eyes were grave. Then *he* walked past her, into the courtyard, looking at me. I knew him by his bejeweled headdress, by his smooth, aloof face, by his cloth-of-gold robes: Shahrazad's eunuch.

I had a strange feeling now in the pit of my stomach. I had wished for him to come, and here he was, standing before me. Yet now . . . I closed my eyes and wished him away. But when I opened them again he was still there. He was staring at my foot.

"Was she this way from birth?" he asked.

"No," Eli said. "It was . . . an accident."

An accident. I felt the shame of it again, the shame so deep that even Uncle Eli, who *never* lied (except to hope out loud) . . . had lied. The old familiar anger washed through me in a wave. I stood still, waiting for it to pass.

"Accident?" The eunuch turned to look at Uncle Eli, raised one eyebrow.

"It happened," Eli said, "before she came to live with us." He didn't look at me. His eyes were avoiding mine.

The eunuch made a sound, an *umm* sound that could mean anything. Then, "Come along," he said to me.

Auntie Chava moved toward me, pressed something into my hand. It was a comb, a jewel-studded comb, the kind you wear in your hair. *Her* comb—the one thing she had saved for herself. "I want you to have it," she said. "I was going to give it to you later, when—" She stopped, then all at once threw her arms around me, enveloping me. I breathed in the smell of her: cumin and citron and a smell that was hers alone. Over her shoulder I met Uncle Eli's gaze. He looked tired, sad. The rims of his eyes were pink.

"But where?" I said, pulling back, fastening my gaze upon Auntie Chava's face. "Where is he taking me?"

"You're going to live there now, Marjan," she said. "In the Sultan's harem. Shahrazad wants you with her and she won't be denied."

"But . . . I don't *want* to live there. I want to live with you."

I half expected her to scold me, for it was not my place to speak out. But instead, she touched my sleeve and said, "Wants don't enter into this, Marjan—save for the queen's wants. We don't want this any more than you."

I gazed numbly about the courtyard—at the threadbare carpets on the floors, at the cracked tiles, at the faded cushions stacked by the wall. It was not nearly as beautiful as the Sultan's harem. And I had to work hard here, every day. But it was a good enough life. Auntie Chava and Uncle Eli, they cared for me. *Loved* me, though they had never said so. Though I was a servant in their home.

I remembered my daydream, how I had imagined that Shahrazad would want my help again. The way it actually happened was not exactly the same. But close. The eunuch. . . I had *seen* him in my imagination, standing in the courtyard, exactly as he stood at this moment. But now I wanted no part of that dream, no part of the brutal life of that harem.

Auntie Chava was wrapping my veil around me. Numbly, I clutched it at my chin. She gazed at me for a moment, then gently traced my eyebrows with her fingers.

"Look to your own survival, child," she whispered.

Chapter 4
Shahrazad's Cripple

No sooner had I stepped within the harem doors than the eunuch handed me off to a bony, beak-nosed woman of middle years. "Follow me," she said crisply, then marched down a wide glazed stairway that ended in a chamber of the baths. She was stripping off my clothes when Auntie Chava's comb, which I had tucked into my sash, skittered across the marble floor. We both knelt to pick it up, but the beak-nosed woman was faster. She turned over the comb in her spindly fingers, darting quick glances at me as if she thought I had stolen it. At last she gave it back—grudgingly, I thought—and was about to rise when something caught her eye. My foot.

She pulled off my sandal and stared. Hot shame flooded my face for the second time that day. I know it's a shock to people, when they first see my foot. How it's stuck turning downward and twisted in, so I have to walk on the inner side of my big toe. How the skin all up the front of it is wrinkly and scarred.

"You're *crippled*," the woman said, and her voice was thin and mean. "Why should she want *you*?"

I didn't answer. I don't know that she expected me to. After another long moment she went on taking off my clothes and then bore them away, pinching them between thumb and forefinger as you would hold a dead rat.

I stood in the center of the vast chamber, naked as a plucked chicken and utterly alone. Far across the room, I could see several towel-swaddled figures reclining on couches. My hands moved to hide my nakedness and I turned my body to hide my foot—though the swaddled women paid me no mind.

It was silent, save for the splash of water. Columns of sunlight streamed in through round holes in the high, vaulted dome. Light mingled with the smoke from burning censers and puddled on the marble floors like liquid gold. Brilliant tapestries, studded with pearls, hung from the walls. At the center of a blue mosaic fountain, four golden lions spouted clouds of glittering spray.

Though I had often been to the Jewish baths with

31

Auntie Chava, they were nothing like this. Not nearly so big. Not nearly so *rich*.

I looked down at the comb in my hand. It was made of silver, with a row of tiny garnets down its spine. Often I had seen it in Auntie Chava's hair. I closed my hand around it—tight. No one would take it from me!

Now I heard the hollow clank of pattens on marble and saw the woman returning. She carried a basket and another pair of pattens. I always have trouble with pattens because of my foot. These were not as high as some— a hand's length from the floor, like foot-sized wooden tables. Still, I knew from experience that it was better to wear them than not. In the inner chambers, the floors were *hot*. I strapped one patten to my good foot and then, feeling the woman's cold, curious gaze upon me, fumbled with the straps of the second until I could drag it across the floor without losing it. Then, "Come," she said, and led the way into the second chamber.

Steam lay dense and warm upon the air. The woman set to work on me, slathering every hair below my neck with depilatory paste, plucking unwanted eyebrow hairs by trapping each one between two crisscrossed strings and yanking—hard!—until tears sprang into my eyes. All the while, she made low, disapproving sounds in the back of her throat. She rinsed off the paste, drawing water from a marble fountain, and scrubbed my scalp and hair. Then she assailed me with a rough-napped glove until my skin felt flayed.

In the third chamber, the air was sweltering hot and so clotted with steam that breathing felt like sucking water. I could hear voices murmuring around me; I could see shadows moving in the mist. The woman led me to a steaming pool and drenched me with near-boiling water. At last, she wrapped me in a muslin bath sheet and herded me back to the first chamber.

Usually, you went slowly through the baths. Usually, you got to relax when you were through washing. When I went to the Jewish baths with Auntie Chava, I would massage the kinks out of her neck and shoulders, and then she would let me lie down. But this woman had hastened from chamber to chamber, and now she did not let me rest. She seated me on a wooden bench and, prodding me to move this way and then that, painted me, powdered me, perfumed me, raked a comb painfully through my hair. Not *my* comb. I wouldn't let her touch it.

But why was she rushing? Where was she taking me next?

I wanted to ask so many things that I couldn't squeeze them all into a single question; they spilled into a stream of questions that started small and flowed out to cover the rest of my life: Would I see Shahrazad soon? Would I be a kitchen drudge or an honored servant? Would I live here forever or would they let me go after a while? Would I ever see Auntie Chava and Uncle Eli again?

I had tried to ask the eunuch, but to no avail. The whole way to the harem I had seen little of him but his back and, when I did catch a glimpse of his face, it was as expressionless as a stick of wood. He did not say a word, even when I asked twice. Even when I asked *loudly*. Now again the questions burned in my mouth, but I chewed them; I did not let them out.

A silky green gown floated down over my head; I thrust my arms through the sleeves. The woman girdled my waist with a length of rose brocade—I slipped the comb inside it—then draped an amber-colored robe about my shoulders. "Open your mouth," she said. "Breathe out." She drew near, sniffed at my breath, winced, reached into her sash and pulled out a couple of leaves. "Chew these." I chewed; mint exploded on my tongue.

The woman stood back, eyed me critically. The fabric slid across my skin—slippery-smooth and far lighter than the coarse muslin I was used to. I felt clean and soft and pretty. But then the woman's gaze drifted down to where my crippled foot, shod in a soft leather slipper, showed beneath the robe; I curbed an impulse to hide the twisted foot behind the sound one.

The corners of the woman's thin mouth turned down. "Well," she said, shaking her head, "you'll have to do."

She moved toward the door, and the question welled up within me, would not be stilled. "Where?" I demanded, not budging. "Where are you taking me now?"

The woman started to say something, then snapped her mouth shut, seeming to consider. At last, she spoke.

"I am taking you," she said, "to the Khatun."

The Khatun.

I had forgotten about her. But it made sense that they would take me to her first.

The Khatun Sultana was the Sultan's mother. The Crown of Veiled Heads. Everyone knew that she was the most powerful woman in the harem. Far more powerful than Shahrazad. Far more powerful than any of the Sultan's wives had ever been—even before he began killing them.

As the saying goes, a man may have many wives, but only one mother.

Another thing I knew about her—she had had three sons. The eldest had been poisoned—killed—by one of the Khatun's jealous co-wives. And I had also heard that the Khatun's third son—this Sultan's younger brother and the ruler of Samarkand—was killing wives every night as well, because his first wife had betrayed *him*. But he had no Shahrazad.

I tried to think what else I'd heard about the Khatun. But it was hard. People didn't talk about her.

I had never, until this moment, found that strange.

Her chamber was dim and cavernous. It smelled of something rotten, sickly sweet. Trying to hide my limp, I followed the beak-nosed woman across dark carpets toward a seated figure in the glow of lamplight ahead. I saw movement in the shadows on either side and made out the shapes of two slave girls wielding long ostrich feather fans. When we drew near, the beak-nosed woman knelt and kissed the floor; I did the same, just behind her.

"Rise." The voice was rough, hoarse, commanding.

The beak-nosed woman stood, moved to one side, and then I could see her clearly.

The Khatun.

She was hugely fat. She seemed to spill over the edges of the massive cushion she was sitting on. Her neck fell in folds over her pearls and I could see the shapes of billowing mounds of flesh beneath her robes. Though her face was bloated, misshapen, it held traces of lost beauty—an arch of brow, a curve of lip. Between pouches of soft, fleshy skin, her dark eyes gleamed.

As she reached with a swollen, beringed hand to motion me near, I heard a tinkling sound. Her gown, I saw, was stitched over from bodice to hem with gems: rubies, pearls, emeralds, diamonds—a staggering display of wealth.

She looked me up and down for what seemed like a very long time. Then, "So," she said in that hoarse voice. "So *this* is the one they told me about—Shahrazad's cripple."

I recoiled as if I had been slapped. Behind her, I heard a stifled giggle. I peered into the darkness and saw a young woman standing there—a beautiful woman with pale skin and coppery hair.

"Precisely what are you to Shahrazad," the Khatun asked, "that she would ask my son to buy you for her?"

That smell, borne on the breeze of the ostrich feather fans, filled my nose—the sweet smell of decay. Smoke rose from incense burners all around, but nothing could mask the stench. I closed off my nostrils from inside—breathed through my mouth—but the revulsion crawled down my throat.

"I . . . don't know, my lady," I said.

I didn't want to tell her. I didn't know quite why; my mind was moving slowly, like wading through a pool of deep water. But I didn't want to tell.

The Khatun held my gaze. For a long time, no one spoke. I was tempted to say something—to babble—to fill the disturbing silence, but I remembered again what Auntie Chava had said: *Chew your words before you let them out.*

"But you must have some ideas on the subject," the Khatun said at last. "The first day you ever came here was yesterday and now—today—you are summoned here to live. Surely you must have *some* thoughts as to why."

I swallowed. Hadn't Shahrazad told her about the mermaid story? Would it be . . . *dangerous* for her to know? I felt as if I were blindfolded, groping my way through a maze full of hidden traps.

"I . . . I was listening to her as she rehearsed her tale for the night," I said carefully. "And one time, when she said that a thing had happened one way, and then later said it happened another, I pointed this out to her."

That *was* true, I thought. And those other women, the ones dressing Shahrazad, had seen it.

The Khatun narrowed her eyes; they nearly disappeared in the folds of puffy flesh. "So, you think Shahrazad wants you for your . . . memory?"

I shrugged, tried to look perplexed. This was too close to the truth for comfort.

"You wouldn't . . . be a storyteller yourself?" the Khatun asked, as if it were an absurd suggestion.

She knew.

There were many in the courtyard who had seen me telling that tale to the children. Someone must have told her. And she could put it together herself that I had been summoned to tell stories to Shahrazad.

I had a sudden inward image of the Khatun sitting in the middle of a spiderweb, a vast web that spanned the whole harem. Any disturbance—anything unusual that happened—would jerk at the web. Make it twitch. And she would know it.

If I played down my skill as a storyteller, she would know I had something to hide. She would know to look beneath my denial for the truth.

So I would . . . exaggerate the truth. Make it outrageous. Laughable. Impossible to believe.

I drew myself up proudly. "I am the greatest story-teller in the city," I said. "Far greater than Shahrazad. If *I* were queen, the Sultan would know the difference between a commonplace tale and a great one."

The copper-haired girl snickered; she had fallen for my trick. But the Khatun had not. She stared at me, and the silence hung between us even longer than before. At last, she spoke.

"I think," she said slowly, "that this *cripple* of Shahrazad's . . . is cleverer than she looks."

Chapter 5
She *Needs* You

LESSONS FOR LIFE AND STORYTELLING

The thing about Shahrazad was, she didn't give up. When the Sultan was killing a new wife every night, and there were hardly any unmarried girls left in the city, and people were getting madder and madder about what was happening to all of their daughters, and it looked as if there might be a revolt, Shahrazad didn't just throw up her hands and quit. She *did* something about it.

I think that's why I admired her so much. Of course, she was clever and learned and beautiful, and she knew how to tell stories in the night. I admired her for those things, too. But the important thing was, she didn't give up.

Unlike my mother, for instance.

The Khatun dismissed me with a wave of her hand, and the copper-haired girl showed me out. Without a word, she led me down a colonnaded hallway to a flight of wooden stairs. She had a showy walk, with a lot of hip in it. Her ankle bracelets jingled, and her long, unbound hair swished from side to side.

I followed her up the stairs and down a narrow hall, past a labyrinth of small rooms—some with curtained doorways, some without. She stopped abruptly, motioned to a faded blue-print curtain. "Your room," she said. "Your clothes are in the chest." She spun on her heel and was gone.

I stood there for a moment, listening to her footfalls as they padded down the wooden stairs and then faded away.

Quiet. It was so quiet. Probably most people had settled down to nap after noon prayers. I hadn't felt so completely alone since they took me away, after my mother . . .

No. I wouldn't think about *her* now.

Tucking the curtain into the bracket beside the doorway, I stepped inside. The room was narrow and dim. A thick blue-and-red carpet covered most of the floor, and an oil lamp stood on a low table near a small wooden chest. By one wall, a copper brazier squatted on the tiles. In the shadowed gloom of the far corner, I could make out a stack of damask cushions and a rolled bed mattress. High on the walls, I saw hooks embedded in the plaster near the ceiling, where tapestries must once have hung.

I knelt beside the chest and lifted the lid. It creaked, exhaled a breath of old, dry roses. There *were* clothes within—folded gowns and veils and trousers of fine silk and muslin and linen. I lifted them out, ran my fingers lightly across them; my rough skin snagged the cloth. Carefully, I held the garments up against my body.

Beautiful. They were beautiful things.

At the bottom of the chest, among a scatter of dry rose petals, lay a frayed prayer rug, a string of plain black prayer beads, and a small prayer stone.

Such *plain* things, compared to the clothes! Plainer than anything I had seen in the harem. A puzzle . . .

Then at once I understood. These were keepsakes brought from home. Some poor girl had been paid for, brought here to the harem, provided with beautiful clothing. The rug, beads, and prayer stone had been all she had to remind herself of home.

A lump rose in my throat. I had not had time to fetch my own prayer beads when the eunuch came to get me. All I had from home was Auntie Chava's comb. I took it out of my sash, turned it over in my hand until the garnets winked in the light from the doorway. Slowly, I set it down in the bottom of the chest with the other girl's things.

The dead girl. For surely she had been killed.

All at once my heart was flooded with longing for my old life—my home and Auntie Chava and Uncle Eli. Why had Shahrazad brought me here? Why couldn't she find someone else to tell her stories?

These fine folk! They played with our lives as if we were tiles on a game board. As if our lives were only of value if we were serving *them*.

I picked up my comb again, slipped it into my hair. There. At least something familiar. Something of my old life. I would wear it now—all the time.

"Marjan?"

Hastily, I shut the chest. I turned round to see Dunyazad in the doorway. My spirits lifted; I felt ashamed of my selfish thoughts.

She moved into the room, then stopped. "I was looking for you; I didn't know where she would put you. You've seen the Khatun?"

I nodded.

"Did she . . ." Dunyazad paused. "Well, never mind. Shahrazad's waiting. Quickly, now.

"She *needs* you!"

Shahrazad's sons were with her: one nearly two years old, another just over a year, and the baby. The infant lay in her lap; the other two snuggled against her like cygnets enfolded in the wings of a mother swan.

She was telling them a story.

Shahrazad looked up and smiled when she saw us enter. But her voice, gentle and low, did not pause. Behind her stood three women—the children's nurses, no doubt.

Dunyazad stopped; I halted just behind her. We watched as Shahrazad finished her tale. Then Dunyazad, signaling me to wait, strode forward. There was much kissing and hugging and cooing and tickling and giggling among the two sisters and the three children, until Shahrazad handed her sons, one by one, to their nurses, and the year-old boy began to wail. The nurses swept past me out the door, and as the wailing thinned and grew faint, I moved forward and kissed the ground before Shahrazad.

"Here, that's enough, sit down," she said. She motioned me to a cushion before her and pressed me to take a handful of honeyed almonds and dates. "The Sultan loved your story, Marjan," she said. "Did you tell her, Sister? How much he loved it?" Shahrazad rocked back and forth on her cushion, her slender arms clasped about another pillow, hugging it to her chest. She was smiling at me, radiant.

"No, I haven't." As Dunyazad settled herself on another

cushion, I was struck again by how different she looked from her graceful older sister. Dunyazad's face was wider, squarer; her body, as she sat, looked solid and compact.

"He had heard that tale when he was a boy," Shahrazad told me, "and he loved it even then. It was one of his favorites!"

"I'm glad!" I said, "but I thought . . ."

"What, Marjan? What did you think?"

"I thought the Sultan didn't want to hear tales he'd heard before."

"He doesn't want *me* to repeat myself," Shahrazad said. "That would be tedious. But he doesn't mind if he's heard some of the tales long ago. In fact, he *likes* hearing his favorite old tales. So, after I finish with the part you told me, he wants me to tell the rest of it."

The rest of it?

"About Julnar's son . . . what happened when he grew up. Shahryar couldn't remember his name. All he remembered was that it has two parts to it, and both parts start with the same sound. A *D* or maybe a *B*—he couldn't recall. He'll be delighted when I tell him."

My heart stood still. *The rest of it.* I didn't know any *rest of it.* I groped back through my memory, trying to remember the name of Julnar's son—trying to remember *anything* about Julnar's son other than the things I had already told, about how he was taken down into the sea as an infant, about the magic that made him able to breathe there. I was *certain* I hadn't heard his name.

Shahrazad was still smiling at me. She looked eager, happy—so different from the day before. I didn't want to tell her that I didn't know what she needed to know. I didn't want to watch her face, how it was going to change.

"Marjan?" She looked puzzled.

I took a deep breath. "My lady," I said. "I am so very sorry. Truly I am. But . . . I know nothing of Julnar's son other than what I've told you. Neither his name nor anything that happened to him after his uncle brought him back from the sea."

A breeze rustled in the curtain that draped the lattice. In the distance, I heard a tinkling of chimes. Shahrazad's face did not change, but rather froze, as if time were no longer flowing, but stood in a quiet pool.

I glanced at Dunyazad, who also seemed stunned.

After a long, long moment, Shahrazad leaned forward, held my gaze. "Are you . . . *certain?*" she asked. "Maybe you've only forgotten, and it will come to you."

I thought back to that day in the bazaar, when I had strayed from Auntie Chava's side and then lost her and wandered from stall to stall until I came upon the blind storyteller. I had listened for a longish while, and then Auntie Chava had found me, scolded me, dragged me away. It had *seemed* as though the tale had ended just when she came. But maybe it hadn't. Maybe he told more of it later—after I had gone.

"I would *know* it," I said, "if I had heard it. I've sometimes wondered what happened to Julnar's son when he grew up. If he ever went back into the sea and breathed there. But—"

Dunyazad leaped to her feet. "The Khatun got to her," she said to Shahrazad. "I *knew* she would." She turned to me. "I think you know—you're just not telling. She threatened you, didn't she? What did she say?"

I was struck dumb. How could Dunyazad *think* that? I had thought that she *liked* me. "She . . . she didn't threaten," I faltered. "Not exactly. She wanted to know why Shahrazad wanted me."

"And you told her, didn't you?"

"No! I didn't even know myself, for certain. But . . . It didn't do any good. To *not* tell her. She knew already."

Dunyazad moved toward me. I shrank away, clambered to my feet, stumbled backward, scattering dates and almonds on the carpet. But still Dunyazad came, until her face was just a finger-length from my own. "You're going to tell us, do you hear me? Everything you know about Julnar's son. Do you hear me? Do you *hear* me?"

"Stop it, Sister." Shahrazad's voice was sharp.

"But she knows!"

"I don't think she does."

"You're too trusting!" Dunyazad wailed. "You've always been too trusting!"

"Sit down, Dunya!" Shahrazad said firmly. "You, too, Marjan. We'll sort this through. Both of you! Sit down!"

Dunyazad set her mouth in a hard little frown, with dimples on either side. But she obeyed with a sudden meekness that surprised me. I sat down, too, carefully covering my bad foot with my gown. And then I had to tell them all about getting lost in the bazaar, about the blind storyteller, about how Auntie Chava had taken me away. I could see that Dunyazad still didn't believe I hadn't heard the rest of the tale. She sat unmoving, with her arms crossed, eyeing me hard.

But Shahrazad believed me—I could tell. "If storytellers in the bazaar are telling of Julnar," she mused, "her story must be widely known. And yet I've never heard of her. She's not in any of my books—"

"Are you certain?" Dunyazad asked. "You have thousands of tales in your books."

"I—like Marjan—would remember," Shahrazad said. "I've read them all and, even though with some it was years ago, the Julnar tale doesn't sound remotely familiar. Besides, sorting through all my books for one particular tale would be like sifting the desert to find a grain of sugar. And we need it *soon*."

"Where did the Sultan hear it?" Dunyazad asked. "Did he say?"

"No. It was when he was a boy. His nurse is long dead. And we couldn't ask the Khatun—"

"Allah forbid!" Dunyazad said.

"None of the eunuchs were here then. Our father—"

"Maybe *he* knows it!"

"Maybe. But I don't know when he'll be back. Since he's traveling with the Sultan's brother, they'll probably be stopping along the way to visit with his ministers in different parts of the kingdom."

Their father, I knew, was the Sultan's vizier. He was in charge of supplying new wives. Auntie Chava once told me that he didn't like this—didn't approve of it at all. But the Sultan had banished his previous vizier for refusing to give him new wives to kill. This vizier—the old one—had been the Sultan's father's vizier and had known the Sultan all his life. The Sultan had trusted him above all other men. So the lesson was clear.

Even less had Shahrazad's father liked the idea of giving his own daughter as a wife to the Sultan. But she had begged him to let her try to end the killings, and at last he had relented.

"I can stretch out the part that Marjan told me for three more nights," Shahrazad was saying now, "but after that . . ."

Dunyazad sighed. "Well, if *she* won't tell you"—she glanced at me—"you'll just have to tell the Sultan you don't know it. Surely he won't . . ." She swallowed. "Surely that will be all right. He's grown fond of you, Sister, I can tell. Just distract him with another good tale. You can get one from Marjan. Unless she refuses to tell you *anything*, and then we'll know for certain whose creature she is."

"I'd be happy to tell you . . ." I stammered. "I know many tales, and I was thinking . . . There are five or six unusual ones that you might not know, and I'd be glad . . ." I trailed off, looking at Shahrazad.

She wasn't listening. She was looking down, hugging her pillow, biting her lower lip.

"What?" Dunyazad asked her.

Shahrazad shook her head.

"Sister, *what?*"

"I . . . I told him I knew it."

"You *what?*" Dunyazad's voice was a whisper.

"Not in so many words. But he told me how he loved the tale about Julnar's son, and he asked me if I would tell it, and he seemed so eager, so happy about it. Like a child he seemed. Like an innocent child." She sighed, gave a sad little laugh, then turned to me. "I was certain you'd know it. Though now that seems foolish. And I led him to believe . . . that *I* knew it. That I would tell it next."

I had the strangest sensation then, as if my heart were cracking in my chest, as if it were crumbling apart like dried clay.

The Sultan abhorred deception. He was famous for it. There was a saying in the city: *like lying to the Sultan*. Eating poison was like lying to the Sultan. Stepping into a nest of cobras was like lying to the Sultan. Plunging a dagger into your heart was like lying to the Sultan.

I had so wanted to help Shahrazad; I had felt so good *thinking* I had helped her. But I had only made things worse.

Dunyazad broke the silence. "When? When did you tell him that? Not when you told the story. Not when I was there."

"When he summoned me later this morning. To see our new son."

"But why did you *say* that? That you knew the rest of the tale?"

Shahrazad shrugged. "He seemed so pleased with me . . . with the baby. And he mentioned the tale again. He asked me straight out if I knew it. I didn't want to displease him. Didn't *dare!* You know that, Dunya, how careful I have to be." She turned to me. "When I tell him certain tales, I must do it in the most delicate way, wrapping stories inside of stories, so he can learn without knowing that I'm teaching. Or at least—without either of us having to acknowledge it. And he's never requested anything from me before now. If I were to refuse him his only request—"

"*Only* request!" Dunyazad cried. "Save that you keep him entertained to his satisfaction every single night, without ever repeating yourself, whether or not you've even given *birth* that day, or he'll—"

"Hush! Keep your voice down, Sister! Walls have rats and rats have ears!"

I cleared my throat; they both looked at me. "Maybe," I ventured, "since it was so long ago when the Sultan heard the tale, maybe he's forgotten exactly how it goes. And I could . . . make up a story about Julnar's son."

Shahrazad looked at me wonderingly. "You can do it

just like that?" she asked. "Make up a whole new story?"

I shrugged. "You can, too."

"For me it's hard. And my stories aren't very good."

"But I'm sure they *are*."

Shahrazad laughed. "I'm human, Marjan—just like you. I'm better at some things than others. But it would be unwise for either of us to make up a story about Julnar's son. The Sultan will know the right one when he hears it. It's like that name . . . the name with the two *D*'s or two *B*'s. When you forget a name like that you don't really forget it, because when you hear it again you know it instantly. It'll be that way with this tale. If you came up with something far different from what he remembers— as you'd be bound to do—he'd be suspicious. *Angry*."

"What about the other women in the harem?" I asked. "One of them must have heard it."

Dunyazad snorted. "*They* won't help."

"They're . . . afraid of the Khatun," Shahrazad said. "They live and die at her whim. So they're very . . . cautious around me."

"Even though my sister's saving all their lives," Dunyazad said. "The young ones, anyway. They're cowards!"

Shahrazad sighed. "Well, things are dangerous for them, too."

"I still don't understand," I said, "why the Khatun—"

"She *hates* my sister!" Dunyazad broke in. "She's a witch!"

"*Shh!*" Shahrazad put a finger to her lips.

"Well she is!"

"If only I could get *out*," I said. "I could find that beggar—I know it. They usually stake out the same places for years." *If*, I added to myself, he was still alive.

"You can't get out," Shahrazad said. "No one can get out."

Dunyazad jolted erect, turned to her sister. "*She* can't get out," she said. "But . . ."

Shahrazad and her sister locked gazes. I could tell they were thinking the same thing. What it was, I hadn't an inkling.

"Don't tell *her*," Dunyazad warned, looking at me. "It isn't safe."

Shaharazad nodded. "Some things are dangerous to know," she told me—though I was sure that was not what Dunyazad had meant. Shahrazad rose, and I stood, too. "Thank you, Marjan," she said, "for all you've done. Can you find your way back to your room?"

"I think so," I said. Dunyazad had taken me by a direct route with no secret passageways—much simpler than the way we had come before.

"We'll speak later," Shahrazad said.

And I was alone again.

Chapter 6

The Terrace

LESSONS FOR LIFE AND STORYTELLING

There are some stories that you don't tell aloud, that you make up and tell silently to yourself. Private stories. You spin them over and over until you don't need them anymore.

I had one about my mother. In this story, she had been brought before the Gazi for judgment. He was asking her questions—hard questions.

I liked to watch her sweat.

I made my way back to my room, stopping at a pool to make ablutions, and then belatedly making up for the noon prayers I had missed. Still quiet. Everyone still resting. It seemed like a week since I had left Auntie Chava, but it was only midafternoon of the very same day. I unrolled the mattress and tried to sleep. I *was* tired—my face ached the way it always does when I haven't slept well or enough. But I couldn't sleep. Sweat beaded on my temples and trickled into my hair. This room, so far from the outside air, was suffocating.

I told myself my story about my mother; sometimes I can sleep after that. But it only stirred up my mind. I kept worrying about Shahrazad—how she was going to get the rest of that story, and if the Sultan would really kill her if she didn't. And what were Shahrazad and Dunyazad planning? "*She* can't get out," Dunyazad had said, "but . . ."

Was she thinking of someone who *could* go out of the harem? Who? A eunuch, maybe? Or a woman who came in to sell trinkets and cloth? Or a man who delivered food for the kitchens?

Some things are dangerous to know, Shahrazad had said. Because of the Khatun.

Was everyone in the harem her *creature*, as Dunyazad had put it?

My glance strayed to the corner where the chest stood in the shadows. The chest with the dead girl's things. Had she been the Khatun's creature? What about all the hundreds of women in the harem who had lived here and been killed—had they been her creatures, too?

What had it been like here, back then, in the old days before the killings? When the harem had been full of women? I got up, opened the chest, fingered the fine cloth of the garments, cradled the dead girl's prayer stone in my palm. I could almost hear the whispers, the pad of slippered feet on the floor. I could almost feel the faint swishing breezes stirred by silk gowns as they passed. I could almost smell the swirling eddies of perfume.

I flung the stone into the chest, shut the lid. This place was haunted! I had to get away!

I couldn't leave the harem, but I could at least get out of this room. Air. I needed fresh air.

I pushed aside the curtain and tiptoed down the hall.

Maybe I could find a courtyard open to the sky. Or a roof terrace. There must be a terrace somewhere.

I didn't know if I was allowed to explore other parts of the harem—but no one had told me *not* to. What harm could it do?

I wandered through a maze of silent hallways lined with closely spaced, curtained doorways. I couldn't resist peeking into one. Slowly, I pulled the curtain aside . . .

Abandoned. Cobwebs festooned the corners; the floor cushions and chest were buried in drifts of dust.

Ghosts.

When you want to find a roof terrace, it's a good idea to look for stairs. I found my way to an open courtyard, then took a wide glazed stairway up. Through a half dozen corridors and stairways and courtyards, I lost my way. From time to time I heard murmured voices behind curtains, and once I heard a child's cry. Then I turned a corner and came face-to-face with two crimson-robed eunuchs guarding an arched doorway. The Khatun's doorway! They stared at me; I whirled around and hurried away.

Though I was relieved that the guards didn't come after me, a deep, aching loneliness was welling up inside. I had come to help Shahrazad, but I had made things worse, and now there was nothing for me to do. No one to help, no one to talk to . . . No one even to sit in the same room with me, to stir the stagnant, perfumed air with breath.

Air. I had to get fresh air.

I came to the end of a corridor, then went down a flight of stairs to yet another courtyard with yet another beautiful fountain. I had seen so many beautiful fountains and beautiful arches and beautiful carpets and beautiful friezes that they were almost beginning to bore me.

Then I caught a glimpse of bright light beyond a wide latticed window at the top of a short stairway. There was a stone parapet, with blue sky beyond.

I ran up the steps—clunking, forgetting to go graceful and silent. I could see it now through the lattice: a terrace. There was a heavy wooden door in the wall; I rattled at the latch, but it was locked.

I peered again through the lattice. In the afternoon sunlight, I could see a graceful pattern of tiles on the floor, and potted flowering bushes, and a haze of trees beyond. The part that I could see was square, but there appeared to be a narrow arm of terrace that stuck out to the left, along the railing. Someone must have been there not long before. A carpet was spread out with damask cushions strewn upon it. At one edge lay a silver tray with glass drinking vessels and a sprinkling of crumbs and seeds.

Maybe it was someone's private terrace. But no one would be outside now, in the heat of the day. And I could *smell* the fresh air!

There were three arched openings in the window lattice, just above the sill, meant to let air and light in—not to let people out. But maybe I could fit.

I hiked my skirts, thrust one leg over the sill and through an arch, then tried to squeeze leg and head and shoulders through the arch at once.

Too small.

I withdrew my leg, then slipped my head and shoulders through the arch, twisting my shoulders. I wormed slowly forward and, giving one last push with my feet, slid through the opening and down onto the hard floor.

The heat struck me like a blow, but the air was washed of the cloying perfume that filled the harem. I breathed in deep and smelled cyprus and jasmine and roses. A light breeze rustled in the leaves of a potted palm tree and tinkled in some hanging chimes.

I got up and walked to the carpet. The drinking vessels, I saw, held traces of sharbats. Someone *had* been here not long ago. Moving to the stone railing, I looked down the narrow arm of the terrace. No one here now.

Below lay a large garden with flowers and fruit trees and blooming bushes. Footpaths wound all through it, leading to ponds with floating water lilies and gilded gazebos. A grove of cypress and boxwood trees at the outer edges cast mottled shadows across the ground.

This must be the garden where the Sultan had caught his first wife dallying with her lover. He had sealed its doorways to the harem, so now only men could go there.

A mournful wail pierced the silence; I looked down to see a peacock wandering along the banks of a pond.

This garden was lovely, but I longed to look out upon the city. I longed to smell the familiar city smells. Sweat and spices and manure. The sharp odor of the tanning vats.

I longed for a glimpse of my old home.

But the view to the city was blocked. Perhaps there were other terraces, higher up.

It didn't matter. I had come to air, away from the ghosts. I fetched a cushion from the carpet and took it onto the arm of the terrace. A flowering vine grew out of a glazed planter and twined up a trellis on the wall opposite the railing. From somewhere above came the soft cooings of pigeons at rest. I set the cushion in the shadow of the wall, leaned back against the trellis, took in a deep breath of jasmine.

My eyelids felt heavy, but I *would* not sleep. I would only rest for a moment.

I jolted awake. I *had* slept! For how long?

The shadow had moved across the floor and had begun to creep up the stone railing.

Voices. Two of them: an older and a younger. One—unmistakable—was the Khatun.

Was this her own private terrace?

What would she do when she found me here?

I sat paralyzed, unable to decide what to do. Then a grating sound—a key in the lock. I jumped up, ran to the far end of the terrace arm.

They wouldn't see me until they came to the railing. But I should show myself now. Surely coming here was no great sin. No one had told me it was forbidden.

The door creaked open; I started to move toward it. The voices grew suddenly loud. ". . . what she's up to," the Khatun said, "with that Marjan."

I froze.

"She *must* have run out of stories. What else could she want with that crippled little monkey?" I recognized the younger voice now. It was the copper-haired girl.

The Khatun laughed, then said more softly, "Oh, there are many possibilities. I'll find out, in good time. My son won't tell me—or he doesn't know himself. He wants to make her *happy*, he says. I don't like it."

"She can't keep up this storytelling forever—can she? She's got to run out of them someday."

The Khatun made a grumbling noise. Then, "When

you're queen," she said, "I'll keep you well supplied with stories."

And then the door creaked again, and there were more footfalls and chattering voices, and a tinkling of silver or glass. But now I couldn't show myself. It was too late, after what I'd heard. *When* you're *queen, I'll keep you well supplied with stories.*

My heart was pounding wildly. I peered over the railing, hoping to find some little outcropping of roof that I could climb down to until it was safe to go back the way I'd come.

Nothing. It dropped sheer to the garden.

"Hsst!"

What was that?

"Hsst! Up here!"

I looked up, craned my neck until I saw her: a crinkle-faced old woman peering at me from atop the roof. "The trellis!" she hissed, pointing at the wooden trellis against the wall. "Climb it! Now!"

I gaped at her. She smiled—shyly, I thought—and motioned furiously for me to come up. *Who was she?*

"Hurry!" she whispered. "They'll see you!"

They'd come and *find* me if they heard her. I looked at the trellis: flimsy-looking crisscrossing slats of wood interlaced with vine. It didn't look sturdy. And the wall was high. If I stayed here and didn't move, no one would see me. I didn't know who this old woman was, or why or *if* she wanted to help me. Maybe this was a trick.

Something moved. A serving woman, coming out from behind the wall. I pressed myself back against the trellis. She said something, and her glance flitted past me. Then she moved back out of sight.

Had she seen me?

I waited a long moment. My bloodbeat rang loud in my ears.

Nothing.

I looked back up; the old woman was gone from the roof. But I couldn't stay here now. Someone *would* see me; it was only a matter of time.

I caught up my fine silk skirts and tucked the ends of them into my sash. Then, clutching the lattice, I wedged my good foot between the slats and pulled myself up. It held.

I tried to climb fast, but the angle of the slats made my bad foot hurt, and my skirts kept tangling between my feet and the lattice, rustling in the leaves. From back on the square part of the terrace, I could hear the Khatun talking and dishes clanking and the wind chimes tinkling, and I prayed that no one would hear me.

I had nearly reached the top when I heard a brittle *crack* and then my bad foot was swimming out in the air and my hand was too—it had slipped off the lattice—and the garden was floating far below. I grabbed for the lattice again; its edges bit into my hands. I groped with my foot for another place to go. There. But would it hold? One hand felt along the edge of the roof for something to grab on to.

Then the old woman was there again, gripping my arm and hauling me up onto a flat piece of roof. My knee hit down with a *thunk*.

"What was that?" I heard from below.

Footsteps. They were coming nearer; they were on the balcony, just beneath us.

"Get behind me," the old woman whispered. "Don't let

them see you." I scrambled behind her, then, "There now, my dear," she said in a high, rich, warbling voice. "Don't flap your wings so loud; the ghosts'll hear you." She was hunched over, facing me, with her back to the terrace, cupping her hands as if she were cradling something within them.

Was she *mad*?

"There, my dear. No flapping. They won't hurt you."

Then from below, a voice: "Zaynab! Get along with you. You know you're not allowed near this terrace."

The woman made a little clucking sound with her tongue. She shooed me before her across the roof.

"Talking to her birds again," I heard someone say down below. "Crazy old Zaynab!"

Chapter 7
Crazy Zaynab

The roof was huge and scary. Most of it was flat, but it was broken up into pieces: a small flat piece over here, a higher flat piece over there, a big square hole that dropped down to a courtyard with no railing and no warning, a cupola, a minaret. Most houses you see use all of their roof space for living. But you could tell that this roof was not made for that. There were no railings round the flat spaces, and the mud surfaces were dirty and unadorned.

Zaynab moved before me like a cat—a plump, round cat—gliding along the flat parts, leaping across gaps, scaling rickety ladders from one level to the next, mincing along ledges, skirting the bases of cupolas. She was amazingly nimble. There was a light springiness to her step, and yet a sort of heaviness in her feet when she jumped that made them land solidly where they were supposed to, without teetering.

I was afraid. The ground looked far below, and sometimes, there was nothing at all between it and me.

"Don't look down!" Zaynab called to me.

But it was hard not to look down. I wanted to see my feet, where they were supposed to step, but often, just beyond the edge of them, was *down*. Down into a tiled courtyard, or down to another level of roof, or down into the garden below.

I hadn't wanted to follow her. She had shooed me away from the Khatun's terrace until we were out of view, then had climbed up a ladder to another level of roof and disappeared. I had stood there, gaping at the rickety ladder, at the space where I had last seen her. She had appeared again—above me. "*Hsst!* Up here!"

I couldn't go back. And I couldn't stay up there all day, on the bare mud roof above the Khatun's terrace. So I had followed, favoring my bad foot—gingerly setting it on the ladder's narrow rungs, scooting it along ledges, walking around the gaps that Zaynab jumped over.

But Zaynab didn't seem to notice my crippled foot or consider that one misstep could plunge me to my death. *Don't look down!* was all the advice she offered.

What was I doing, following a crazy woman across this treacherous roof?

But I thought of the Khatun and kept going.

At last, as I was hauling myself up another ladder, a small, circular pavilion arose before me on a tiled rooftop terrace. The pavilion was made of yellow bricks, with a domed roof and a row of slender, arched windows all the way around. Nearby, flowering bushes and trees sprouted up from clay pots. Bird droppings speckled the floor, growing denser and denser toward the far end, where I saw three pigeon lofts—thatched mud huts shaped like cones. They were pierced with clusters of small round holes, with sticks poking out beneath. Pigeons peered out through the holes, perched on the sticks, preened on the loft roofs, and strutted on the low wall that edged the terrace. From within the lofts welled up the rich, peaceful, burbling sound of many contented birds.

When I turned around, Zaynab was looking at me; she quickly averted her eyes. A pigeon sat on her shoulder, pecked at her gray hair. Her robes were mottled with telltale white streaks. "Would you . . ." Again she seemed shy. "Would you like a cup of sharbat?"

It would have been rude to refuse. I followed her into the shade of the pavilion.

The carpets, scattered about the floor, were faded and frayed and littered with feathers. White droppings splotched the tiles. It smelled musty. Of *bird*. Yet it was a fine room, with designs in green and brown tiles on the floor and in purple and blue on the high ceiling. Like earth and sky, I thought.

Humming a tuneless tune, Zaynab poured water into a bowl and hastily scrubbed two clay cups. The wash water turned chalky white. Bird droppings in the cups? It seemed likely, because now two more pigeons flew in and joined the one pecking at Zaynab's hair. I watched warily as she ladled sharbat from an earthenware jar. Still, she didn't seem really *crazy*—except for the reckless jaunt across the roof and the birds on her shoulders and that imaginary bird she had talked to. Unless you counted terrible housekeeping as a sign of craziness. Which Auntie Chava probably would.

Who *was* this Zaynab? I wondered. What did she do here? Why had she saved me from the Khatun? Or . . . *had* she saved me?

"Here you go, my dear," Zaynab said, handing me a cup of sharbat.

My dear. That was what she had called the imaginary bird. Still, the sharbat looked clean enough. I had half feared to find a feather floating in it—or worse. Sipping, I found that it was sweet and good.

I smiled at Zaynab. "This is delicious," I said. "Thank you."

She nodded, smiled, ducked her head, then quickly turned and scattered some seeds on the tile floor. The birds on her shoulders fluttered down and began pecking; four or five new pigeons sailed in through the windows and joined them. Zaynab sat staring at the pigeons, humming softly to herself. Abruptly, she broke off and looked at me.

"Do you like views?" she asked.

"Views?"

"The view," she said. "Over there. We can look. If you want. You don't have to unless you want to."

"I'd like to," I said.

We crossed to a window and silently looked out. The whole city lay before us—beige flat-roofed buildings, studded with bright domes and spindly minarets. The sun, low in the sky, cast long shadows and bathed the highest points in golden light. To the east, like a deep blue silk scarf, lay the river. And beyond, along the horizon, stretched a row of green hills. My mother had grown up beyond the green hills, I suddenly remembered.

The boats and carts and buildings looked tiny from here. Like toys. Much tinier than they had looked from Auntie Chava's terrace. Toy people jostling in the streets. Toy donkeys and toy camels. A toy herdsman with his flock of toy goats.

I tried to find the pathway through the city that would take me to Uncle Eli and Auntie Chava's home. But everything looked different. I could recognize a few landmarks—the tanning pits, the domed roofs of the bazaar, the minaret of a nearby mosque—but I couldn't piece the whole city together and make sense of it.

Nor could I make sense of the palace roof. The harem, I knew, lay in the middle, but where? I found the garden with the cypress and boxwood trees, but try as I might to match the bumps and hollows in the roof to places I knew, I could not.

Zaynab was looking off into the distance, still humming. I waited in vain for her to say something—anything.

Through the window screen, I caught a glimpse of the pigeon houses. Something I had once heard . . . "Do you . . . keep the messenger pigeons?" I asked.

Zaynab cut off her humming abruptly. "I and my grandfather before me."

I sipped my sharbat, searching for something else to say, hoping that *she* would say something. But she was humming under her breath again. Then she said as if to herself, "Pigeons are easier than people."

What could I say to *that*? I tipped back my sharbat, finished it. "I . . . should be going back to the harem. Is there another way down . . . besides . . . um . . . besides . . ." Now *I* sounded like the crazy one. But Zaynab rescued me from my own awkward tongue.

She took my cup and led me out to the terrace. "This way." She pointed to a long, narrow stairway that wound down into darkness. "You'll come out near the harem kitchens. The door is unlocked." Zaynab paused, then added, "I would be glad . . . if you would visit me another day."

"Thank you," I said. But I didn't think I'd come. Zaynab was *strange*.

I was nearly past the first curve when Zaynab called down to me. "Marjan?"

I turned back. Sun streamed all around her into the dim stairwell.

"Watch out for the Khatun. She's not your friend."

It wasn't until I was back inside the harem that I realized I'd never told her my name.

Dunyazad came to see me in my room after evening prayers. It was hard, now, talking to her. She was careful, polite. But there was none of the warmth that I had felt from her before. None of the *liking*.

She wanted to know how to find the storyteller in the bazaar, and I told her as well as I could, though I didn't remember exactly where he had been. Somewhere near the carpet bazaar, by a fountain. It had been a long time ago. I had been *lost*. Also, he might have changed places. Or moved to another city. Or *died*.

I wanted to let her know what I had overheard, about the Khatun preparing the copper-haired girl to take over Shahrazad's job. Although I didn't know how to do it. Dunyazad would wonder how I knew, and the truth was odd enough that she might be suspicious. I told her anyway.

She just looked at me. Then she said, "Might as well get a *donkey* to tell him stories."

So, I thought, after Dunyazad had left, I must have guessed right about what she and Shahrazad were planning. They would send someone to look for the storyteller. Someone who could come and go in and out of the harem. Someone—I hoped—with a good memory. You can't send just anybody to get stories and have them do a good job.

But if he couldn't find the storyteller . . .

A sick, sinking fear dragged at me. He *had* to.

If he couldn't . . .

Dunyazad would think I was to blame. She would think that I had lied to protect myself from the Khatun. She would think I didn't care what happened to Shahrazad, since the Sultan would never marry *me*.

She didn't know me at all.

The next morning, right after dawn prayers, I lighted my lamp and made my way toward the corridor that led from Shahrazad's quarters to the Sultan's bedchamber.

For once, I was not alone. Flickering lights, all moving in the same direction, drifted through the dim courtyards and hallways—an odd, silent pilgrimage. I recognized the beak-nosed woman who had taken me to the baths, and a woman who had bought one of Auntie Chava's brooches, and a few of the children who had listened to the story of the fishes. I followed them to a courtyard staircase that led up to the alabaster corridor I had seen that first day. A cluster of people—fifteen or twenty, I guessed—sat or stood in pools of light on the wide marble steps. There was the gazelle girl with her pet, and the copper-haired girl. There were two eunuchs: one old and bitter looking; another young, with a sad, gentle face.

You would think that women gathered in this way would talk—to gossip or exchange confidences or simply pass the time. You would think that children would have trouble holding their tongues. But this group was strangely hushed.

I stood at the rear, near the bottom of the steps. No one seemed to notice. But then the young eunuch with the gentle face turned round to look at me. And smiled.

Was he Shahrazad's ally? I wondered. The one they were sending to find the storyteller?

But now there was a shifting in the crowd, a sigh. I looked up to see the gold-clad eunuch walking toward us, moving through the arch. With Shahrazad and her sister behind.

She lives! My heart gave a glad little leap.

Shahrazad turned and smiled. A public smile. A queen's smile. Her glanced skimmed over the crowd; she didn't seem truly to *see* anyone. I was hoping that she would smile especially at me. That she would . . . what? Thank me in front of everyone? Summon me to her quarters?

But she didn't.

She moved with her sister through the arched doorway and into her rooms.

When I looked about me again, the steps were empty. Just a few people remained in the courtyard. As I watched, they disappeared through one arch or another until only the gazelle was left. He sniffed at the air, took a hesitant step, then pranced lightly across the square. When he vanished through an archway, I stood listening to the echoing clicks that his hooves made on the tiles.

They didn't summon me that day. And all the time I worried: Had they found the storyteller? If they had, did he know the rest of the tale? Shahrazad had said she could stretch out the part I had already told her for three more nights. Now only two were left. If she didn't have the tale . . .

Dread clung to me like a damp gown. I wished there were something I could *do*.

I went for a long walk through the harem to keep myself from going crazy. No one stopped me from exploring, and soon I could find my way around. The lived-in parts were scattered throughout the harem and parceled out—I guessed—according to where people stood with the Khatun. Her favorite servants—the copper-haired one and the beak-nosed one—lived in magnificent suites of rooms. Women with children seemed to have more than one room as well. But most of us lived in tiny rooms, even though many fine ones stood empty. And, aside from the Khatun and her favorites, no one lived very near to anyone else. It seemed as if the Khatun was trying to keep the rest of us apart.

But the children didn't want to stay apart from me.

Three of them found me after their midday naps and pestered me to tell them a story, then more children appeared as if by magic as I spun the tale. It was one I had made up. I decided to try it, see how it went. When I finished, a boy who had come in late began to beg for another story. Then they were all begging, even the gazelle girl. She even offered to let me pet her gazelle. I told them three more stories—including another one I had made up. I attempted some of the voice-and-body things Shahrazad had done, but I couldn't do them half as well. The children were begging for more when their mothers shooed them away, saying I must need a rest.

But I truly didn't mind.

The next day just after dawn, I again watched Shahrazad emerge from the Sultan's quarters. Alive! But only one more night remained of the Julnar story.

And still she didn't summon me.

Was that a good sign? Or bad?

The children found me earlier this day and pestered me even longer for stories. When my voice grew hoarse and I told them to come back the next day, the gazelle girl—her name was Mitra—followed me about, talking about her pet, telling me the names of everyone in the harem and what she thought of them, until her aunt called her away.

Even so, I had plenty of time left over to worry that afternoon. Nothing much *happened* in the harem, other than the morning pilgrimage to see Shahrazad. You could hear the moazzen calling for prayer three times a day. Twice a day, food appeared in my room. I had never seen who brought it; I was always wandering.

My mind went round and round about Shahrazad's

dilemma and I was filled with an ever-growing sense of helplessness and doom.

At last, after afternoon prayers, I returned up the spiral kitchen stairway to Zaynab.

I still couldn't make up my mind about her: whether she was crazy or a spy for the Khatun. But that terrace— away from ghosts and conspiracies, away from the perfume- heavy air of the harem—drew me.

She didn't seem surprised to see me. She looked up, blinking, when I came out of the stairway, and her face lit with a smile. She was holding a pigeon cupped in her hands; as I watched, she released it into the air. I gazed at the bird sailing over the tiny toy city and felt, just for a moment, that all my cares and worries and grievances were but toy things, too, and that life was truly peaceful and safe.

Zaynab *did* talk to her birds, I found. But it didn't seem crazy.

It seemed as though they *listened*.

Chapter 8

On the Wrong Side

Late in the afternoon of my third day in the harem, Dunyazad appeared while I was telling the children a story and summoned me to her sister. I had to break off in the middle. When the children complained, I told them they would have to be like the Sultan and wait for the next day.

I couldn't tell from Dunyazad's expression whether they had found the story or not. She seemed guarded, her emotions carefully veiled. She didn't trust me anymore. But one look at Shahrazad's face told me everything.

They didn't have it.

"We . . . couldn't find him, Marjan," she said, as I rose from kneeling at her feet. "We don't know if we were looking at the right fountain, or . . . Might he have moved from that place?"

"It's . . . possible," I said. Though entertainers usually staked out the same spots for years, they did *sometimes* move.

"My sister . . . she has an idea."

I turned to Dunyazad. She was looking down, away from me, as if she were studying the pattern of the carpet.

"She wanted to go with you," Shahrazad said, "but I forbade her. It will be . . . dangerous."

She waited, then, silent. *Dangerous.* As if I would object to a thing because it was dangerous. As if *she* hadn't faced danger every night for nearly three years.

"Just tell me what it is," I said, "and I'll do it. I would do anything for you."

The next morning, after the moazzen's call to dawn prayer, Dunyazad came to fetch me. I was expecting her. We had gone over the whole plan the afternoon before in Shahrazad's quarters. Now Dunyazad didn't say a word, only put her finger to her lips, signaling me to hush. She peeked out into the hallway; I followed her down the stairs and into a small wood-paneled room. Gently, she pushed on one of the panels. A soft *click*. The panel became a door that swung silently in toward us.

She motioned me through the opening, into darkness. I turned to watch as she came in after, as she grasped a latch on the door and pulled it shut. Then I couldn't see anything at all.

I felt her moving past me, breathed her perfume. It

smelled fresh, like rain. Then she took hold of my wrist and tugged me behind her through the passage.

I was afraid that my bad foot would thump too loudly on the hard stone floor. I was afraid that I would trip and fall. I ran one hand along the wall for balance—I felt wood, then stone, then wood. Dunyazad let go of my wrist, and now I could just barely see the back of her. We turned a corner; light seeped in through a carved sandstone screen in the wall. When we had passed, it grew dim, then dark again.

It was like that in the passage. Tar black, and then dimly lit when we came upon screens of wood or sandstone, or metal grillworks, or odd little cutouts in the walls that must, I thought, be part of designs on the other side.

I kept wishing for a lamp, but of course we couldn't use one. It would shine through the holes; people might see us going by. Anyway, Dunyazad seemed to have memorized these dark passages with her feet.

Unlike the first day she led me through the hidden passages, we didn't go in and out of the main part of the harem. Dunyazad went fast, still—too fast for my liking. But now she grabbed my wrist from time to time and steered me.

At last, she stopped. It was in one of the dark places; I ran into her with an "*oof!*" and then whispered that I was sorry.

"Shh!" she said. I could hear her fumbling at something, and then a click, and there was a crack of light down low that grew into a square. We crawled—Dunyazad first, then me—through the small, low doorway into Shahrazad's suite.

Shahrazad came forward to greet us, motioning us to

be quiet. I kissed the floor at her feet and, rising, saw the chest behind her, the one they had spoken of the day before. It was the size and shape of a small coffin, made of dark-varnished rosewood, with a deep, complicated design carved on its lid. One of its hinges had twisted and pulled away from the wood, and a long, raw scratch scarred the front panel.

"It saddened me to do that," Shahrazad said, looking at the scratch. "I've always liked this chest. But . . ."

But if the chest weren't damaged, she couldn't send it out of the harem for repair.

Shahrazad handed me a pair of sandals and a veil—a fine full-length black veil, made of heavy slubbed silk. It made me uneasy, the veil. It would mark me as a rich woman. And rich women, though they might go to the bazaar from time to time, would have male relatives and eunuchs with them.

"Do you have . . . another veil?" I asked her. "One not so fine?"

The sisters exchanged a glance. "It's mine," Dunyazad said. "It's the least fine one I own."

Now Dunyazad embraced her sister and made for the hidden panel door. She stooped to go through it, then turned back to me. "May Allah keep all hateful things from you," she said. I couldn't read in her voice whether she truly meant it or not. Then she disappeared into the passage; the panel clicked shut behind her.

Shahrazad was opening the chest. "I put pillows inside," she said. "I got in myself to see how it would feel. You can breathe; some of the carving on the lid goes all the way through. Do you see?" She pointed to a pattern of holes on the inside of the lid. A moment before, with the lid closed, I had not seen that they pierced it through. "My legs were cramped," Shahrazad went on, "but you're not so tall as I. Anyway, you won't be in there long. The cabinet-maker's shop, they tell me, is not far. And remember, they'll come to pick you up before sunset prayers. They lock the harem gates at dusk. Don't be late, Marjan—no matter what! Oh! and . . ." She reached inside her sash. "I almost forgot. Here." She put three heavy gold dinars in my hand. I gaped at them. "Isn't that enough?" she asked.

I was about to tell her that in fact, they were far too much. These dinars would draw attention to me, draw *suspicion* to me. Copper fils would be better, with maybe a silver dirham or two. But before I had a chance to say it, she dropped two more dinars into my hands, saying, "Better too many than too few."

A loud knock at the door; I jumped.

"Hurry!" Shahrazad whispered. "Get in!" She pushed me gently toward the chest.

I thrust the coins into the folds of my sash. Quickly, I climbed inside and put on the sandals. I couldn't straighten my legs. But when I bent them, lying on my back, and put my feet against the end wall of the chest, it wasn't uncomfortable. Shahrazad tucked a pillow between my head and the wall of the chest and covered me up to my neck with a narrow carpet. "So no one can peer through the holes and see you," she said softly. She lowered the lid, then lifted it again—just a crack—and I was staring up into her eyes.

"Thank you, Marjan," she said.

Knocking again. The lid came down, and I heard the metallic clinking of a key in the lock of the trunk.

A wild rush of panic surged up inside me, and for a

moment, it was hard to breathe. I resisted the urge to call out, to push at the lid.

And then I remembered a story I had heard about a boy who was imprisoned in a copper bottle by magic. He calmed his fears by imagining he was a silkworm in its cocoon. So I imagined that *I* was a silkworm, too—safe and snug in my own cozy home. No one could see me here. No one could harm me. I gulped down a deep breath—it smelled of sandalwood—and felt my panic ebb.

It was dark in the chest, though not completely. Light trickled through the cluster of holes in the lid.

I could hear low, muffled voices. The barest hint of Shahrazad's perfume lingered in the sandalwood-smelling air. Then there were footfalls, coming this way.

I braced myself, pushing my head against one end, my feet against the other, my hands on either side. "The important thing is that you don't move," Shahrazad had said the day before when she had explained the plan. I had asked her if the bearers wouldn't know, from the weight of me, that someone was in the chest. She told me that the chest itself was so heavy, they wouldn't know the difference. And she told me not to stir.

All at once, the chest was hefted into the air with little jerks and sways and lurches. I heard the sounds of fabric rubbing against wood, and labored breathing, and soft bumps as the chest hit against something. Someone's leg. It would have to be a eunuch's. None of the harem women would be strong enough to carry the chest, and tradesmen would never come inside Shahrazad's rooms. In my mind, I pictured the young eunuch, the one who had smiled at me. Might *he* be one of the bearers? Might he be the one who *knew*?

Now we were going down, though the chest was level, not tipping. They must be walking side by side down the stairs. Then the sound of splashing water: the courtyard.

Soon, I lost track of where we were. There were too many ups and downs, too many turnings this way and that. It had grown hot inside the chest. Before long I heard a loud creaking noise—a gate, I thought—and then the sounds of the street rushed in. Shoutings. Cart rumblings. Cloppings of hooves on stone. Beyond the fragrance of sandalwood, I could smell the street—sweat and animal fur and manure. All at once, my feet lurched upward and my head pressed hard against the pillow. The bottom of the chest was scraping against something—a cart? A shrill, rasping noise. A clunk. For a moment, all was still.

Then we were moving again—a different kind of moving. Something rumbled beneath me—it *must* be a cart—with quakes and jostles, sudden sharp jolts. I was *very* hot now. A bead of sweat trickled off my forehead into my hair.

I tried at first to imagine where we were going, which streets we were on, but before long I was thoroughly confused. And I didn't know where the shop was that they were smuggling me to.

Smuggling. Like the outlaw who smuggled girls out of the city so that they wouldn't become brides of the Sultan. Abu Muslem was what they called him; nobody knew his real name. My mother had spoken of him, but she hadn't *done* anything about it. If she had done the right thing, I would have been safe and whole.

At last, the cart stopped. I heard that same shrill rasp—the back gate hinge of the cart, I guessed. I braced myself. The chest dropped suddenly—I heard the grunt of an exhaled breath—then I was carried for a short distance and set down upon something solid and flat.

Footsteps, moving away. The sound of a door shutting.

Then nothing. I could hear street sounds, but they were muffled, faraway sounding.

I waited.

Hot. Sweat streamed off my face into my hair. My back was soaked.

Was this the cabinetmaker's shop?

Little light seeped in through the holes in the chest lid, so I must be in a shaded place. I breathed in deep, trying to see if I could *smell* this place, and I thought I caught a whiff of varnish.

Suddenly, I heard footfalls. There was the clinking of the key in the lock, and then footfalls again. Running away.

Shahrazad had told me that someone would come to unlock the chest at the cabinetmaker's shop. But she had said that they would help me out of the chest, that they would point me in the direction of the bazaar.

I waited awhile longer. All quiet.

Why didn't someone open the lid?

Was it safe to get out?

Still quiet.

At last, I could bear it no longer. I pushed back the carpet and slowly lifted the lid of the chest. Just a crack. I could see a clutter of trunks and chests and cabinets and tables. Beyond, hanging on the wall, I could make out the shapes of woodworking tools.

No one there.

I opened the lid and clambered out, pulling my veil

over my head and holding it securely under my chin. My legs felt stiff and a little bit numb. My bad foot ached. I stretched out, looking over the rest of the room—a small, dark room with heavy drapes drawn across the windows. The door had been left ajar.

Still no one. Why was there no one here?

All at once it struck me that no one had spoken on my whole journey here in the chest. The bearers in the harem had not spoken, and the cart driver had not spoken, and again, since I had arrived here at the cabinetmaker's, I had heard not a single voice. People *would* speak when they shared a task. They would say, "I'll go first," or "I'll take up the rear." They would comment on the heaviness or the lightness of the chest, or they would greet someone working nearby.

They didn't want me to hear them. They didn't want me to see them. They didn't want me to know who they were. No one wanted to be connected with any secret goings-on at the harem. You could die for that, if you were on the wrong side. And going against the Khatun . . . *put* you on the wrong side.

I shook off the thought. What was important was finding the storyteller. I *had* to find him. Today. Otherwise, Shahrazad would die.

I crept to the door and peered out into the brightness. A courtyard. Empty, save for the cart and one lonely palm tree in a patch of dirt near the wall. The gate leading to the street was ajar.

I moved to the tree, scooped out some dirt in one hand and rubbed it into the splendid slubbed silk. There. Now it didn't look *quite* so fine.

I walked briskly to the gate and let myself out.

Chapter 9

The Bazaar

LESSONS FOR LIFE AND STORYTELLING

There are many schools of thought on how to pick a ripe melon. The thumpers give a sharp rap and listen for a hollow sound. The sniffers claim they can nose out a ripe melon by smell. The gazers judge by color—a yellow hue beneath the fine, pale netting on the skin of the fruit. (But this only works for muskmelons.)

My auntie Chava taught me to inspect the scar at the stem end. If it is well callused and sunken just enough, the melon will be good and sweet.

I came out in a deserted, narrow alley, lined with walls and doors. A little way to my left, the alley ended in a stone wall. To my right, some distance away, I could see a street—a busy street—cutting across the alley. I memorized the look of the wooden door to the cabinetmaker's courtyard—how it nestled in the arch of the wall, how its white paint had begun to peel at one corner. It was the third door from the end of the alley. I could remember that.

I made my way to the street and put memory to use again, fixing the intersection in my mind—the green door on one wall, the metal grillwork of a high window across the street.

The crowd flowed in a great, strong river to the left, with only a few trickles moving right. So I went left, too. I didn't recognize this place, but I knew that most people would be going toward the bazaar. I threaded my way among pack mules and merchants, through groups of women carrying bundles on their heads, between a band of musicians and some important dignitary being carried on a litter. Soon, not far ahead, I could see the high, open-sided domes of the bazaar.

The bazaar was huge, and I knew my way about only parts of it, and not the part where I had seen the blind storyteller. He had been near the carpet bazaar—but where? I tried to picture the fountain—the one I had told Dunyazad about. There weren't many fountains in the bazaar. It shouldn't be hard to find.

I headed through the narrow shop-lined streets toward the carpet bazaar. It was not far from the food stalls, I remembered. I knew that place well, for I had gone there many times to shop with Auntie Chava.

I cut through the crowd—ducking this way to avoid a swinging elbow, darting that way to dodge a heavy boot, slipping into short-lived pockets of space as they opened up in the throng before me.

Light and dark washed over me as I moved through patches of hot sunlight into cool, welcome stretches of shade—a domed arcade, a stone arch that spanned the street, wide canopies jutting out from the shops, a roof of hanging shawls strung overhead from one side of the street to the other.

And everywhere there was noise—merchants crying

their wares; street musicians playing horns and lutes and drums; mule drivers cursing; women haggling; caged birds screeching; brass workers' mallets pinging and clanging and bonging. Smells drifted past: sawdust, perfume, leather, dye, feathers, manure—all mingled with the ever-present odor of sweat.

Now, just ahead, I could see the food stalls: the fruit sellers, the spice sellers, the grain sellers. I pushed through the crowd of women—women thumping melons, women squeezing eggplants, women inspecting pomegranates for bugs. I moved past buckets of fresh fish, baskets of cheese, heaped mounds of spices in rough hempen bags. I breathed in the familiar smells of this place: ripe fruit and briny olives. Raw fish and pungent cheeses. Cinnamon and cumin, jasmine and myrtle, saffron and cloves.

Every other time I had been here, I had been with Auntie Chava. The smells nearly conjured her up.

I glanced about me, feeling a sudden, sharp surge of hope. Just to *see* her . . .

Searching, I moved through the crowd. I looked for her face; I watched the swaying movement of long veils and robes for her walk; I listened through the clamor for her voice—complaining that the quinces were bruised or the price of dates disgraceful. I would *know* Auntie Chava. I knew her by heart.

She wasn't there.

At last I stopped, let the river of people wash past. An emptiness opened up inside me. I knew it wouldn't have been good to see her. She would be worried to find me here, outside of the harem—and beside herself when she found out what I was up to. But still . . .

Now, beyond the baskets of lentils and shelled almonds, I could see carpets. A whole row of them, hanging on a line strung above the street from one side of the domed arcade to the other.

I moved into the carpet bazaar, peering into every stall and staring at the beggars who sat against the walls. My bad foot clunked against something hard—a wooden loom. The carpet weaver yelled out a curse, ceased her knotting, and shooed me away. I hobbled down the street; my foot *hurt*. Worse, this didn't seem quite like the right place. The street was too narrow. There had been a crowd gathered around the storyteller, but here there was no *room* for that.

At last, through a gap in the mass of bodies before me, I glimpsed a high spurt of water glinting in the sun.

A fountain.

I pressed through the throng, faster now, until I came to a wide, open place where two streets crossed. And there, like an island in the middle of the moving river of people, was another crowd. A still crowd, in front of the fountain.

Listening to a story?

I wriggled between the bodies until I could see what they were watching . . .

My heart sank.

It was a man with a performing monkey.

I looked past him, at the fountain. Water splashed down into a blue-and-gold-tiled basin. It was the same fountain—I was almost certain.

So where was the storyteller?

Panic bubbled up within me; I pushed it down. This didn't mean he wasn't *here*, I told myself. Maybe there was another fountain in the carpet bazaar. Or maybe he had moved to a different place. It had been a long time ago, after all. I had been *lost*, after all.

I squeezed backward through the crowd, then stumbled through the carpet bazaar, searching. The sharp pain in my foot had eased, but now it ached with every step. Here was another place where the street widened. But no fountain. No still crowd of listeners. Then, to my left, I saw a flight of stone steps, leading down. And I remembered: There was more of the carpet bazaar below.

I hobbled down the steps, jostling against shoppers, trying to keep my balance, then moved through the cool, dark lower part of the bazaar, through yellow scraps of light where the sun streamed in through holes in the vaulted ceiling.

Nothing. No fountain. No storyteller.

The panic was pushing up again.

Stairs. More stairs.

Hobbling up again, past lacy, wooden screens and men who worked lathes with their feet. I rounded a corner into the leather bazaar with its revolting stench of animal skins and the blistering reek of the tanning vats.

And always I looked for the blind storyteller. I saw fortunetellers and snake charmers and water sellers and lute players. Once, my heart leaped into my throat as I heard the thread of a story, saw a crowd standing around a seated man. But I knew as soon as I saw his face that he was not *my* storyteller.

At last, hot and sweaty, I found myself back among the food stalls. My bad foot ached and throbbed. The inner side of my big toe burned where it pressed my sandal straps against the ground, and the whole bottom half of my leg had seized in a cramp. I leaned against a wall and massaged my leg. The day had grown hot, and flies swarmed in great buzzing clouds about the food. About *me*. The thick commingled reeks of spoiling fruit and overripe cheeses and animal droppings made my stomach roil. My mouth was parched. I looked longingly at the water seller, squirting thin, cool jets of water into the brass cups that dangled from the harness on his chest. But the only money I had was the gold dinars Shahrazad had given me. And gold was too dear for a cup of water. People would stare and become suspicious. I'd be a target for thieves.

As much as I admired Shahrazad, I began to see that she knew little of the world outside of the harem. To make a mistake like that . . . And now I felt uneasy about this plan. A plan for the outside world, made by two people who had never seen it. All hinging on this storyteller, a man I had seen but once, years ago. Who might have moved to another city by now. Who might have *died*.

If only Auntie Chava were here! She knew the whole bazaar as well as her own front courtyard; she would know how to find the storyteller.

But . . . I could go to *her*. I could ask her where the blind storyteller had been. And then I could see her. Could talk to her.

I imagined what it would be like to go home. How happy Auntie Chava would be to see me. Old Mordecai would open the courtyard gates and she would look up from her work, then she would run to me, and—

What was that?

I started up out of my daydream. A crimson robe, like most of the harem eunuchs wore. Two of them.

I crouched down, watched them pass. Their faces

were blocked; I couldn't tell who they were. But I knew they came from the harem.

Were they looking for me?

And I knew it then, that I couldn't go to Auntie Chava. It would be dangerous for her to know what I was doing. Because if the Khatun had discovered that I was gone, she would send her men to Auntie Chava's home and have it searched. They would question Auntie Chava. They might already have gone there. And someone would wait there . . . for me.

I pressed myself back against the wall, the panic rising in a thick, choking wave inside me. The storyteller was gone! How could I have imagined he would still be here after all these years? I had been foolish even to think it!

I would never get that story, and Shahrazad would have to tell the Sultan that she had lied, and then . . .

Then she would die. The Sultan would marry the copper-haired girl who told stories worse than a donkey, and then more women would die. And the city would go back to the way it had been, with unmarried girls living in terror for their lives, and their fathers and brothers threatening rebellion.

But right now I didn't care about that. Right now I cared only about Shahrazad.

"Move aside, girl. Move aside."

I stumbled out of the way of a short, hunched woman, who unrolled a small rug and sat down upon it. The fortuneteller. I remembered her from when I used to come here with Auntie Chava. This was her spot. The woman fanned a deck of cards and called out for people to have their fortunes told.

I'd like to know *my* fortune, I thought. But I couldn't use the dinars.

And then I realized: If I had looked for the fortuneteller earlier, she wouldn't have been here. People came at different times. I couldn't remember what time of day it had been when I had seen the storyteller but . . . maybe he *did* still come to the bazaar, only later. How could I have been so stupid, not to have thought of this?

With new hope, I made my way back to the fountain. I walked carefully, hiding my limp, and kept my head down in case the eunuchs were still about. The man with the monkey had gone and now there was just the crowd hurrying through streets in the harsh midmorning sun.

I saw down on the edge of the fountain to wait.

He didn't come.

A band of musicians—two horn players and a drummer—set up and played for a while. Then a mule driver led his animals to drink in the fountain. A water seller passed by, ringing his bell and calling out that his water was cold and clear. I felt my gold dinars through the cloth of my sash. Too risky. So I cupped my hands and drank from the fountain—away from where the mules had been.

A moazzen called for noon prayers. Most of the bazaar emptied out as people went to pray and then to sleep during the hottest part of the day. I found a cool, dark place in the underground part of the carvers' bazaar, behind a heap of sawdust. There was no place private to make ablutions with water, so I made ablutions touching earth and said my prayers. I curled up to rest—but I couldn't sleep. Worry gnawed at me more and more.

Later, when the bazaar began to come back to life, I made another trek all through it, even down to the tanning vats. I saw no more harem eunuchs, to my relief. When I returned to the fountain, the fortuneteller had set up there.

Still no storyteller.

Shadows crept into the streets. The sun had moved overhead and to the west. Precious time was passing. Where was the blind storyteller?

Dread seeped into my heart.

I glanced around at the merchants and carpet weavers. From looking at them half the day, I had begun to know their faces. Maybe they would know the storyteller.

I didn't want to ask. I didn't want to call attention to myself. But I had to do something.

I approached one of the merchants, a stout one with a full, curly beard. "Uncle?" I said.

He looked at me as you would look at a beetle before flicking it off your sleeve; but then his glance snagged upon the fine cloth of my veil. Now he smiled; a broad row of teeth opened up in the middle of the brush.

"Do you know . . . Does a blind storyteller ever come here?" I asked. "To tell stories by the fountain?"

The smile vanished. He turned away from me and began straightening a pile of small carpets. "I don't know," he said.

"But surely you would—"

"*I don't know,*" he barked. "Now, unless you've come to buy, be on your way!"

I asked many people in the stalls all around, and it was always the same. They did not say *no*, that they knew of

88

no blind storyteller. But they averted their eyes, and said, "I don't know."

"Sister?"

I whirled round to see a boy before me. By his frayed robe, I guessed he was some poor man's servant.

"I know the man you speak of," he said. "He's not here today. He is not . . . feeling well. For seven copper fils, I will take you to him."

Chapter 10

A Name with Two Words

The boy grinned at me then, a crooked, impish grin. He was taller than me, but probably around my own age. His face was smudged with dirt, but his eyes were amazing—huge and dark, with thick, long lashes.

I had seen his type before. A charmer.

"How do I know that you know him?" I asked, suspi-cious.

"He wears a peacock feather on his turban," the boy said. And I could see it, then, that feather, bobbing this way and that as the blind storyteller told his tale. Excitement rose within me. "Very well. Take me to him," I said.

The boy held out his palm. "Payment in advance."

"No. I don't pay in advance," I said.

"Very well, then, half."

"I can't give you half. I'll pay you well when I see him."

The boy didn't move. "How do I know you have money?"

I tried to sound haughty. "Believe it. I do."

He said nothing—just kept his palm out.

I sighed. I would have to show him a gold coin. I reached into my sash and pulled one out. Eyes wide, he grabbed for it. I snatched the coin back and tucked it into my sash. "Let's go."

The boy shook his head. "I don't know you," he said. "How do I know you'll pay?"

"I don't know you, either!" My voice sounded shrill, even to me. I looked about quickly. A few people had turned to stare. More quietly, I asked, "How do I know you won't just run off and leave me?"

The boy grinned that grin of his. "You don't," he said. "You'll have to trust me."

If I gave him the coin, he would disappear and I would never see him again. I stood firm, shook my head.

The boy shrugged, but I saw the hunger in his eyes. Hunger for the gold dinar. "Well then, come along," he said.

I kept my eyes on the tattered, grimy back of him as he wove through the crowds in the street. It was hard to keep up because I was trying not to limp, in case the eunuchs were still about. People kept cutting between us, getting in the way. I bumped into one woman and stepped on another's foot; they shouted at me, shaking their fists. Just when I thought I had lost the boy, I caught sight of him leaning against a pillar, waiting for me. "This way," he said, and again he was off.

I followed him all through the bazaar, and then into a part of the city I didn't know. The courtyard walls turned from brick to mud; the streets narrowed and the crowd thinned out; the paving stones gave way to packed earth. Dust rose in puffs from our footsteps, filling my nose with grit.

I gave up trying to hide my limp. It had been a long time since I'd seen the eunuchs, and my foot was hurting again. The boy drew farther and farther ahead, until once, when he looked back at me, I saw a startled look cross his face. After that, he slowed down. Though I didn't want his pity, I was glad for the slower pace.

I clung to hope. The storyteller had looked poor; he *would* live in this part of the city.

We went so far and so long and by so twisted a route that I began to think the boy had led me in circles—like some porters who, paid by the distance they carry a foreigner's goods, take the longest possible way.

Well, this boy would be far overpaid!

Then he was gone.

I stopped, waiting for him to appear from around a corner. The courtyard gates, tightly spaced in the cracked mud walls that lined the narrow street, had only traces of paint and hung crooked on their hinges. These homes must be tiny. All was deserted, save for three dirty children and a skinny chicken pecking in the dust. I had no idea where I was.

"Boy?" I called.

Nothing.

He had abandoned me.

I couldn't *believe* he had given up that dinar, and yet . . . "Boy!" I called again.

One of the children pointed at my bad foot; the others giggled. I turned away, angry at the children, angry at the boy. He hadn't known where the old storyteller lived; he had only wanted my money. When I didn't give it to him, he punished me by leading me on a wild chase until I was utterly lost.

How could I have allowed him to trick me? I, who knew my way about this city. I, who was carefully schooled by Auntie Chava in not letting people take advantage.

Probably the old beggar had died long before, and his story with him.

My bad foot was throbbing again. My knees felt weak; I let them fold. I sank down into the dirty street, put my head down on my knees. I felt numb. What I wanted to do more than anything was to make my way somehow back to Auntie Chava's house and enfold myself in her arms.

But I couldn't.

"Sister?"

I clambered to my feet. He was there again, the boy. "A thousand pardons, Sister. If you'll just let me tie this about your eyes . . ." He held out a red kerchief, moved toward me.

My relief turned to anger. A blindfold!

"You don't know who sent me," I said. "If you did, you wouldn't humiliate me like this."

"I don't care who sent you. I'm not taking you to the storyteller unless you wear the kerchief."

I wanted to walk away. But I *needed* that story.

The boy turned, started to leave. "Very well," I said quickly. "Take me to him! And don't dawdle about it!"

As he tied the cloth over my eyes, I told myself that I was crazy to let him do this. Far crazier than Zaynab. Probably he belonged to a band of brigands. They would beat me and rob me and leave me to die on the floor of some wretched hovel.

"Don't try to rob me," I said. "You don't want to make enemies of my friends."

I heard something—it sounded like a snort. Was he laughing at me? I couldn't tell. Still, even though I knew what I was doing was crazy, the hope wouldn't go away. "Hope makes crazy fools of us all," Auntie Chava sometimes said.

I kept my free hand pressed against the coins. The boy took my elbow. He led me gently enough. We walked slowly, and he warned me when we were going to turn, or when there were steps to go up or down, or when there were animal droppings near my feet. At last, I heard a creaking of hinges—the boy led me forward a little way—then more creaking as the door closed behind us. Someone was fumbling with the kerchief; it fell from my eyes and there, sitting on a faded carpet at the far end of a small, bare, mud-walled room, was the storyteller.

I knew his face at once. I had watched it intently for a long time that day—the high forehead; the shaggy brows that arched up to sharp points; the wild, frizzled beard, now grown more white than gray; the thin, papery skin that crinkled round his eyes. But there was something different about him, something that took me a moment to place. No peacock feather. But that wasn't it.

His eyes. When I had seen him before, they had been unfocused, roving. *Blind*, I had thought. But now they were sharp, piercing, intelligent.

"I don't know you," he said. "Who *are* you?"

We had rehearsed this part, Shahrazad, Dunyazad, and I. I was not to tell him anything, just ask for the story.

"It doesn't matter who I am," I said. "I'm looking for a story. A *certain* story. I heard you tell the first part in the bazaar, about a mermaid called Julnar. Now I want to hear about her son."

"Julnar," the man said, and a smile twitched his mouth. "When did you hear about Julnar?"

I started to reply, then thought better of it. "It doesn't matter when I heard it," I said. "I'll answer no questions—but I will pay you well."

"I've no doubt of it," the man said.

"Here," I said, pulling a dinar out of my sash. "This is for the story. There's another for you when you're done."

I expected him to snatch it from me. But he made no move to take it—just left me there, holding it out, feeling foolish.

"Do you remember the story?" I asked.

"Yes."

I set the coin down on the carpet. Still the man did not pick it up. This was a hovel they lived in—I could tell by the carpet and the walls and the tiny packed-dirt yard outside the window. So much money would pay for the storyteller's food for a year. *More* than a year. I remembered how, in the bazaar, he would stop with the telling until he heard the encouraging clank of a coin in his cup. But now he ignored it. He gazed just over my left shoulder, combing his beard with his fingers.

And I felt a twinge of fear. I had thought him a poor, blind, harmless old storyteller. But I began to get the feeling now that he was much more than he seemed.

"Sister?" The boy was staring at the coin as a starving man would stare at a leg of mutton. I almost felt like laughing. He turned and held out his hand. "Where's mine?" he asked. "You promised."

I let out an exasperated breath, pulled out another coin. He snatched it, bit it to see if it was real, then tucked it away.

"So," the storyteller said at last. "You want to hear about Badar Basim."

A name with two words, both starting with a B!

I nodded, trying to look calm. *Badar Basim,* I said to myself. *Badar Basim.* I moved forward, not wanting to miss a single word.

Chapter 11

I *Always* Find Out

LESSONS FOR LIFE AND STORYTELLING

I always used to like stories that had justice in them. Stories where the right people got punished. In my favorite stories, if something bad happened to you in the end, it was because you clearly deserved it.

My auntie Chava used to tell me that it's not like that in real life, and I shouldn't expect it to be.

But I knew that already. Because I didn't ask to have a crippled foot . . . and I didn't do anything to deserve it.

It was growing late. Shadows stretched across the yard, but the storyteller never paused.

Badar Basim had been shipwrecked trying to go home; now he was in the ocean, clinging to a plank.

"A thousand pardons," I said, interrupting the flow of the tale. "But I have to be back . . . home. By sunset. Are you nearly to the end?"

The storyteller raised his shaggy brows. "There is *much* left to tell," he said.

I needed all of it, and yet . . . I had to get at least some of it back to Shahrazad in time for her to learn it and tell it *tonight*. "Then I'll have to come back," I said. "Can I find you by the fountain? Tomorrow? Or the next day?"

The man combed his beard with his fingers, seeming to take thought. "Ayaz"—he nodded at the boy—"will go by there every morning and afternoon. Wait there, and he will find *you*."

Ayaz grinned crookedly and held up his accursed kerchief.

He removed it in the same place he had put it on, in the street near the crumbling walls. The crowds thickened as we approached the bazaar, until they were as dense as they had been that morning. Ayaz walked more slowly than before. The sun was sliding down the sky, and shadows flooded the streets.

He left me by the fountain where he had found me. I watched him slip through the crowd and disappear. Then I threaded my way—running!—through the narrow streets.

I chanted to the rhythm of my footsteps: *Badar Basim, Badar Basim*. Then I was through the arch to the carvers' bazaar and into the street.

My foot began to ache again. I had a stitch in my side, and my breath came fast and hard.

At last I saw them, the high metal grillwork first and then the green door. I cut through the crowds, nearly getting stepped on by a camel, then veered into the alley and hurried to the cabinetmaker's gate.

I knocked, but no one answered. I pushed; the gate yielded. It was open.

The courtyard was deserted. Still.

I crossed it, slipped through the open doorway to the shop. Even though the light was dim, I found it at once among the bulky shapes of chests and cabinets and shelves: *my* chest.

It was open.

I climbed in, adjusted the pillows and carpet, pulled the lid down over me. I lay in the dark, still breathing hard. Sandalwood. It smelled good.

Hurry, I thought. Sunset will come fast.

In a moment, I heard footfalls from the direction of the door. I heard the rattling of the key in the chest's lock, and then felt myself being lifted.

A grunting breath. Thumpings of boots on tile. The gritty feel beneath my back of the chest sliding across a wood surface, then the shrill rasp and thunk of the cart gate closing. And I was moving again, jiggling, jolting.

I could hear the creak of the wheels, the *clop* of a mule's feet, voices in the street. But they were muted. There was a kind of quiet inside the chest. I thought about the storyteller's tale, trying to engrave it in my memory: How Badar Basim had fallen in love with Princess Jauharah, but because of a family quarrel, she turned him by sorcery into a beautiful white bird with orange legs and a red bill. How the princess commanded her slave girl to take Badar Basim to a barren island to die; but the girl, Marsinah, feeling pity for him, took him to an island with many trees and fruits. How another enchantress returned him to his true form, and the king of that land fit him out with a ship and crew. Then the shipwreck, where the storyteller had left off . . .

I would have to be careful to remember everything exactly as the storyteller had told it, and not let the tale veer off in a different direction. It was a rich, exciting tale. But something bothered me about it—how Princess

Jauharah had betrayed poor Badar Basim, when he loved her so well. It echoed too nearly what had happened to the Sultan himself with his unfaithful wife.

What if the story encouraged him in his belief that all women were betrayers? What if he became angry, thinking about it again? What if he took it out on Shahrazad?

There was more, the storyteller had said. *Much left to tell.* The blind storyteller . . . who was *not* blind. Could I have remembered him wrong?

Also strange was the fact that he had shown no interest in gold. A poor man like that.

And another thing. Where had he gotten the tale? A tale that Shahrazad had not heard before and was not in any of her books. And yet one which the Sultan had known since he was a boy.

It must, I reassured myself, be a tale told among men, and had not been told widely enough to reach women or books.

But even more worrisome: Was it the *right* tale? The one the Sultan wanted?

There was no way to know for certain until Shahrazad told it to him tonight.

And yet, it had seemed right. It connected with the Julnar story.

And the name: Badar Basim. I repeated it over and over in my mind, clutching it to me like a talisman.

At last, we came to a halt. I was hot again. Sweating. I could hear voices, and then a clapping of hands. More voices. Eunuchs' voices. I heard the cart gate creaking open, and then I was moving; the chest grated against the cart floor and I was lifted into the air, borne silently aloft. This time, I didn't even try to imagine which stairway we were going up or which fountain I heard. Soon, I told myself, I could tell Shahrazad that I had found the old storyteller. I could hardly wait to see her face when I said the name: *Badar Basim.*

The chest clunked down on the floor. I heard footfalls receding, and then a faint, close, rattling sound. Now another set of footfalls, moving away.

"Who's there?" Shahrazad's voice, at a distance. Then, "Dunya! Come here! The chest!"

More footfalls now, soft and light, coming near. "Where's the key?" I heard Shahrazad say. "The key's not here."

A shadow passed over the holes in the chest. "Marjan?" Shahrazad asked. "Are you there?"

"Yes," I said. "I found the storyteller."

"Oh! Allah be thanked, Marjan!" Shahrazad said. "But . . . where's the key?"

"I don't know," I said. "I heard it being locked, in the cabinetmaker's shop. And then—"

I stopped, remembering the faint rattling I'd heard a moment ago. "I think," I said, "one of the eunuchs took it."

"One of the eunuchs?"

"One of the . . . bearers. I heard a rattling just before he left."

The shadow moved away from the top of the chest. "Send for him!" I heard Dunyazad say. "You've got to get it back!"

"But why would he take it?" Shahrazad asked. "Unless . . ."

"The Khatun!" Dunyazad's voice. "He's taking it to *her.*"

Footfalls, leaving the room. A shadow fell across the holes in the chest again. "We'll get you out soon," Shahrazad said. "Don't worry."

But *she* sounded worried. My breath was coming fast

and scared. I was hot now, *really* hot. The air in the chest felt suffocating.

"Did you get the name?" she asked.

"Yes. Julnar's son was . . . Badar Basim."

"Badar Basim!" She whispered the name, as you would say the name of a loved one. "A name with two words, each beginning with the same letter, a *B* or a *D*. Badar Basim!"

Footsteps. "Here's Dunya, Marjan. We'll have you out soon."

I could heard Dunyazad saying something. Her voice came fast, excited. But I couldn't understand her. Then, "*Now?*" Shahrazad said. "She's on her way *now?*"

There was a frantic rattling in the lock. "We couldn't get the key, Marjan," Shahrazad said. "Dunya's going to try opening it with a midak. The Khatun . . . she's on her way here."

More rattling. Hurry, I thought. *Hurry!*

"They're coming!" Shahrazad's voice. "They're at the top of the steps!"

A click, and the lid flew open; light flooded in. Hands were reaching down to me, helping me up, pulling off the carpet, my veil, straightening my gown. I stumbled over the edge of the chest—my legs were stiff. Dunyazad pulled me to stand beside her, and then there they were: Ashraf, the woman who had taken me to the baths. Soraya, the copper-haired girl. The gold-clad eunuch, looking sterner than ever. And behind them all, borne on a litter by four out-of-breath eunuchs, the Khatun.

The eunuchs, sweating and straining, set down the litter. Ashraf and Soraya helped the Khatun heave her massive bulk from the chair.

That smell again. That rotten smell.

Shahrazad moved to greet her. "My lady," she said, bending to kiss the Khatun's swollen hand. Shahrazad was so smooth, so poised, you would never have guessed that she had been desperate moments before. The Khatun lurched past her, peered into the chest. She picked up the carpet I had used from where it lay bunched on the floor, then flicked her fingers at the eunuchs. They moved through Shahrazad's rooms, searching behind curtains and under cushions, opening cabinets and cupboards—but not, I saw to my relief, the hidden panel door. The Khatun watched, her eyes small and hard, squeezed between pillows of flesh. When the eunuchs had finished, she turned to Shahrazad. "How did you open the chest?" she rasped.

"Something seems to have happened to the key," Shahrazad said. "I didn't want to bother you, and so . . ." She picked the midak off the floor. "We opened it with this."

Auntie Chava had a midak, a long needlelike instrument for threading a sash through the waistband of a pair of trousers. But *hers* was not made of ivory and capped with gold.

"They did a nice job repairing it, don't you think?" Shahrazad pointed to the place where the scratch had been. It had vanished completely. The cabinetmaker must have worked for hours.

The Khatun glared at Shahrazad, fury in her eyes. She turned her fierce gaze on Dunyazad, then on me. Sweat was streaming off my face; she couldn't help but notice.

She turned back to Shahrazad. "Don't bother lying," she said, "because I'll find out.

"I *always* find out."

Chapter 12
I Forbid It!

LESSONS FOR LIFE AND STORYTELLING

When you're telling a story, you can suggest things that would get you in trouble if you were just stating your own opinion. And you can suggest even more if you wrap one tale inside another. So if you're telling a tale about a merchant, and the merchant tells a tale about a barber, and the barber tells a tale about a fisherman . . . Well, inside the fisherman's tale you can put the most provoking and mutinous truths. Because the tale is so far removed from you.

That's what Shahrazad did. Wrapped up morsels of truth in a confection of tales, which she served to the Sultan each night. She was hoping that in time those truths wouldn't seem mutinous anymore—just *true*.

"Do you think she knows?" Dunyazad asked, after the Khatun and her servants had left.

We were sitting on cushions on the floor. Shahrazad hugged another pillow, rocking back and forth, biting her lip. Thinking. She shrugged. "She couldn't know for certain."

"She was suspicious, though." There was a look in Dunyazad's eyes that I hadn't seen before. She was afraid.

"She must have been, or she wouldn't have come here. When's the last time you saw her leave her rooms?" Shahrazad sighed. "And I'm sure we *looked* suspicious. But she can't prove anything."

"If they saw Marjan getting out of the chest . . ."

"I don't think they did. I think she was . . . *just* out when the Khatun got to the door." Shahrazad turned to me. "Did they see you getting out, do you think?"

"I don't know," I said. "I was . . . hurrying. I couldn't tell." Now that the Khatun was gone, I noticed that I felt a little weak. A little shaky. She *scared* me.

"I wonder what she was looking for," Shahrazad said slowly, "when she sent the eunuchs to the bazaar. And I wonder why that eunuch—or whoever it was—gave her the key in the first place?" She looked at Dunyazad and then at me, raising her brows as if expecting us to answer.

We couldn't. We didn't know.

Shahrazad brightened suddenly and turned to Dunyazad. "Marjan got the story!" she said. "We'd better get started."

"Not all of it," I said. "There wasn't time."

"There's . . . *more?*" Shahrazad's smile melted from her face.

I felt terrible. If only I'd asked about the storyteller before noon prayers, and if only Ayaz had heard me, and if only he had taken me to him before most of the day had passed! I told Shahrazad and Dunyazad what had happened and that I had learned enough of the story to last more than one night.

"So we're going to have to do this again," Dunyazad

said to her sister. "It's going to be harder, now the Khatun's suspicious. She's always hated you, but now . . ."

"Why—" I began. How could *anyone* hate Shahrazad?

She looked up. "Why what, Marjan?"

"Why does she *hate* you?"

"Because my sister's not a spineless little puppet," Dunyazad said.

Shahrazad shrugged. "The Khatun does like people she can control. But I think there's something else that goes back to when her sons were growing up. They were always in danger of being assassinated by her husband's other wives, so that *their* sons would become Sultan. Her oldest son was poisoned—you've heard about that?"

I nodded. It had happened a long time ago, before I was born. But everyone knew about it.

"They put ground glass in his milk. It was horrible. So the Khatun . . . became a tigress. She was ferocious. She protected her remaining two sons against so many women when they were young that she doesn't trust any woman to get close to them now. She's always suspecting plots."

"You're too charitable, Sister," Dunyazad said. "That woman is evil."

"The important thing," Shahrazad said, "is that Marjan has some of the story. Tell me, Marjan! Time's running out."

She leaned forward as I told it; I could see the eagerness in her eyes. Dunyazad paced about the room. When I had finished, Shahrazad began to rehearse the tale herself—as she had done that first day. She learned it quickly. "This is a wondrous tale," she said. "And it *will* last for two more nights. Maybe three."

"What about . . . the betrayal?" I asked. "How Princess Jauharah tricked Badar Basim. Might that not—"

"No—it's fine," she said. "But I will need the rest of it. This blind storyteller. You can find him again?"

I nodded. I began to tell her how Ayaz had led me to him. But partway through, Shahrazad broke in. "Dunya, what's the matter?"

"What if . . ." The fear was back in Dunyazad's eyes. "What if this story . . . isn't the one the Sultan wants?"

Shahrazad looked puzzled. "Why wouldn't it be?"

Dunyazad turned to me. "This storyteller," she said, "was *not* where you found him before?"

"Well no, but . . . I *recognized* him," I said.

"Six years later, and you're certain you remembered? He couldn't be another old man, pretending to be blind?"

"You worry too much, Little Sister! Why would he do that?"

"For gold! Marjan was asking for this story, and the boy saw a way to part her from her dinars, so he took her to someone who *claimed* to be the blind story-teller."

"But he *wasn't* blind," I said. "He . . ."

Now I felt *both* of their gazes heavy upon me. "I only *thought* he was blind before. But it was the same man. I knew his face like . . ." I appealed to Shahrazad. "Like the Sultan will know the name of Badar Basim when he hears it."

I hoped that Shahrazad would reassure me, because we had had this conversation before. About how you could forget things, but then know them instantly once you heard them or saw them again.

She nodded, but looked uncertain. "This story does . . . *fit* with the other one."

"It's a loose fit, Sister. It's completely different from Julnar's story. Practically the only thing they have in common is that they're about merfolk."

"So you're saying . . . This old man may have made up a tale to trick Marjan into paying him. That it might not be the one the Sultan remembers?"

"And the name," Dunyazad said. "That's what he wanted, wasn't it? The name."

"Badar Basim," Shahrazad said. "That could be wrong?"

Dunyazad shrugged. "I don't know. Did you tell him," she asked me, "that you were looking for a name with two words starting with a *B* or a *D*?"

"No," I said. "Or . . . I don't *think* so." She was confusing me. I tried to remember. I didn't think I had said anything about that.

"The Sultan is very particular about names," Dunyazad went on. "He's *unreasonable*. Remember when you forgot that one name, just after little Nasim was born? And I remembered it just in time? He looked *angry*. If the story is completely different, and if the name is completely different, might he think . . . that you never knew it to begin with? That you told him you did, and then you made something up? It's just . . . The right story would confirm his trust in you. But the wrong one . . ."

"Would make him *doubt* me. But you recognized this man," Shahrazad said, turning to me. "He was the storyteller. You *remember* him. You can tell me that for certain?"

I hesitated. I had thought that I did, before Dunyazad's questions. But now . . .

Still, I would not have told him about the two words and the *B* and the *D*. I was certain I would not. And I *had* felt that burst of recognition when I saw him. That knowing.

I nodded.

"Lady?"

Shahrazad's women stood at the door, the women who prepared her for her nights with the Sultan.

"Go, Marjan," Shahrazad said softly. "I have the tale here." She tapped her temple. "I'll see you in the morning."

I only hoped that she would.

All night long, my mind churned. I went over and over everything that had happened with Ayaz and the storyteller—especially the part where the old man had told me Badar Basim's name. I hadn't said anything about the two words and the *D*'s and the *B*'s—I was certain. Well, nearly certain. Yet Ayaz *had* seemed eager to get those coins. And he *had* disappeared and left me in the street before coming to fetch me the last bit of the way. There had been time for him to prepare the old man.

And there was something else as well, something that had been niggling at me but which hadn't come to the surface until now. I had said *blind* storyteller when I'd asked about him in the bazaar. And no one had said, "There is no blind storyteller." They had only averted their eyes and said, "I don't know." As if they were afraid. And Ayaz. He must have heard me say *blind*, but he had taken me to a man who could see.

If Ayaz and the old man had been bent on deceiving me, why hadn't the old man pretended to be blind?

But if he *was* my blind storyteller . . . how was it that he could see?

I was already awake the next morning when I heard the moazzen calling for dawn prayers. His cry sounded thin and sad; it made me ache for home. When I had finished my prayers, I made for the stairway near where Shahrazad would appear.

Walking down the hallway, I thought I heard the pad of bare feet behind me. I stopped, turned back. The hall was empty. But the curtain to one of the rooms rippled, as if stirred by a mysterious breeze.

Uneasy, I hurried to the stairway.

The usual gathering was there: a scattering of children, six or seven women, a few eunuchs. I didn't see the copper-haired girl, Soraya. As I stood at the back of the group, little Mitra came up beside me. Her gazelle nuzzled at my hands; I scratched the bony place between its horns. One by one, the other children drifted down the steps; soon they were all clustered around me.

I wondered if anyone here knew that this was not an ordinary morning—that this past night had been more perilous for Shahrazad than other nights. I glanced at the young eunuch, but he was turned so I couldn't see his face. Then I caught movement at the far edge of the courtyard. Soraya appeared in an archway, climbed the steps, and sat down beside Ashraf.

Now, at last, the door was opening. I held my breath. And there she was, walking with her sister behind the gold-clad eunuch.

Shahrazad.

A sigh arose from the crowd. I let out my breath; my whole body sagged with relief.

Shahrazad was looking toward the steps. When her eyes found me, she stopped, smiled, and signaled me to *come*.

"It was just as he had remembered it," Shahrazad said. She was still smiling, radiant. Dunyazad had left on an errand; Shahrazad had sent away her serving women and now sat by me on a cushion on the floor.

"He hadn't remembered all of it," she continued, "but when I told the tale, he said it was like meeting an old friend. And Badar Basim! The Sultan joked with me that I had tortured him, making him wait those several nights to relieve the itch in his mind. But he didn't hold it against me—so long as I had the name."

I tried to imagine the Sultan . . . *joking* with Shahrazad. But I couldn't. It was too far to reach. I had watched him riding somberly in processions through the streets, and twice I had seen him striding through a courtyard in the harem. His face looked . . . hard. Dead. Like stone. And . . . with everything else I knew about him . . . Joking!

"I was worried," I confessed, "about Princess Jauharah. Because . . . Badar Basim was in love with her, and she betrayed him."

Shahrazad looked at me for a moment. "And you were afraid," she asked, "that this story would give the Sultan further proof that all women betray the men they love? And he might be inclined to have me killed? Is that it?"

I nodded.

"He *knows* there are betraying women in the world, Marjan! So the tale tells him nothing new of that. And if I omitted all women like that from my tales, he would know that I was shading the truth. That I was . . . lying, in a way. About how the world is. And Jauharah is not *all* bad. She's false to Badar Basim in order to be true to her father. And besides, there's Marsinah, the kindly slave girl who saves Badar Basim. And Julnar herself, who is strong and good."

"Yes, I see that. But—"

"Marjan. I have told him tales of good women and bad

111

women, strong women and weak women, shy women and bold women, clever women and stupid women, honest women and women who betray. I'm hoping that, by living inside their skins while he hears their stories, he'll understand over time that women are not all this way or that way. I'm hoping he'll look at women as he does at men—that you must judge each of us on her own merits, and not condemn us or exalt us only because we belong to a particular sex."

I began to get a glimmering, then, of what Shahrazad had meant when she spoke of *teaching* the Sultan. And my awe of her grew. She was not simply saving her own life—saving many women's lives—by telling entertaining tales. She was . . . educating the Sultan. Enlarging his view of the world. Giving his bitter, cramped soul room to grow. Making him . . . *human* again.

"Anyway," she went on, "you can't just go chopping off the parts of a story that you don't agree with and scrubbing the rest of it clean. You violate its spirit. You rob it of its power. You—Sister! There you are!"

Dunyazad entered the room. She smiled her dimply smile at Shahrazad, then turned and smiled at *me*. Maybe she trusted me, now that the story had gone well.

When the door had shut tight behind her, she asked, "Did you tell her?"

Sighing, Shahrazad shook her head. To me, she said, "I asked the Sultan where he had heard the tale, but he looked off into the distance and didn't answer. We were hoping we could learn the rest of it some other way. So—I'm sorry, Marjan. But—you'll have to go out again."

"I know," I said.

"But I don't think you'd better go out in a chest. Or come back in the same way you go out."

I nodded fervently.

"And this time," Dunyazad said, "I'm going, too."

You would have thought, by the way Shahrazad acted next, that Dunyazad had said she was going to jump off the highest minaret in the city. And it *was* a crazy idea. But Dunyazad was stubborn—even stubborner than Auntie Chava sometimes gets. "I forbid it," Shahrazad kept saying. "I absolutely forbid it."

"I have ways of getting around your forbiddings—as well you know," Dunyazad replied.

Shahrazad sighed. "Listen to *reason*, Little Sister. If the Khatun doesn't scare you, think of this: Father has enemies. They might use you to get to him. They might—*hurt* you to punish him. And *Father* would be your enemy should he ever find out. Likely he'd marry you off to some toothless, doddering old landlord, and I'd never see you again! And think of me! If anything happened to you, I wouldn't be able to say I need to tell my little sister a story. Shahryar would have to admit that the stories are for *him*. And he might be too proud for that."

"But I have an idea!"

"Of course you have an idea! You always have ideas! And sometimes you even have good ones. But this is reckless, Sister! It's madness! Marjan, tell her she's mad."

"Um," I said. I couldn't say *that*. "It would be . . . easier . . . with just me."

"No—no, wait!" Dunyazad said. "My plan calls for two, and there's no one else to do it. Here's what I want to do. You know how Princess Budur dressed up as a man and no one knew?"

"Princess Budur! Dunya, Princess Budur is not real.

She's a girl in a *tale*! People in tales do all kinds of crazy things. They turn into birds and donkeys. They fly on toy horses and get into shipwrecks. That doesn't mean *you* should do them."

"But, Sister, you're the one who taught me that there is truth below the surfaces of tales. That we can learn courage from them. That they can teach us how to live our lives."

"Don't go twisting my words around! This is crazy and you know it. I forbid it."

"So *you're* the only one who gets to be brave and heroic. Brave Shahrazad. The savior of all the women. And I have to be meek and obedient. Little meek Dunya. Isn't she lucky to have such a brave, heroic older sister!"

Shahrazad struggled to hold back a smile, then gave up and, laughing, said, "No one ever called *you* meek, Sister."

An answering, dimpled smile flickered across Dunyazad's face. "Well, maybe not. But if we don't do this, the Sultan will be angry and chop off your head, and I won't be far behind. Preserving *you* will save me."

"Not if you get yourself killed first. I forbid it."

"Sister, I am doing this! With your permission or without. So what do you plan to do about it? Send for Father to marry me off to a toothless old landlord—"

"I'm tempted!"

"—or help us, so we won't get caught?"

Chapter 13

She Should Have Been Strong

There were many wrinkles that had to be pressed out of Dunyazad's plan.

One was the part about dressing up as boys. Dunyazad had fallen in love with the idea, but it didn't make sense. "Girls can get along in the outside world just as well as boys," she said. "Princess Budur proved that when she dressed up as her husband and nobody knew the difference. She even *ruled* and nobody knew."

"I'm glad you were listening," Shahrazad said, "but her situation does not apply to you. In the first place, she's a made-up person. In the second place, you need to be as covered up as possible, which means veiled, which means dressed as a woman, not a man."

Eventually, Dunyazad saw reason and gave up the idea. I was glad. *I* didn't want to go traipsing through the city unveiled.

Another wrinkle was those footsteps I'd heard that morning on my way to see Shahrazad. "You're certain you're being followed?" she asked.

"I *think* so," I said.

"Do you know who?"

"I didn't see but . . . I think it may be Soraya."

Dunyazad jumped up, pushed open the door, and went out. She returned in a moment. "It *is* Soraya. When she saw me, she fled down the stairs and ducked into a room."

"Hmm." Shahrazad bit her lip, looked thoughtful. "We'll have to do something about that."

Yet another wrinkle was the part about *both* of us leaving the harem. Dunyazad was even more in love with this idea than with the dressing-as-a-boy idea. But Shahrazad wouldn't allow it until we came to the next wrinkle.

Which was: How could we make sure that this would be the last time either of us had to leave the harem? Once had been bad enough. But *twice*. Far more dangerous, because now the Khatun was suspicious. This next time *had* to be the last.

"How much more of the story was left?" Shahrazad asked. "Did he say?"

"He said . . ." I tried to remember. "Something like . . . 'There is *much* left to hear.'"

"More than he could tell you in a morning? In a day?"

"I don't know," I said. "I guess I should have asked."

Shahrazad rocked on her cushion, hugging a small satin pillow. "That makes it hard."

For a moment, no one spoke. Not even Dunyazad had an idea.

Then I thought of Zaynab and her pigeons. They

were trained to return messages to the palace. If the storyteller had some palace pigeons, he could send back bits of story.

"Ah!" Shahrazad said, when I told her what I was thinking. She turned to Dunyazad; they exchanged a long, meaningful look. And I felt . . . cut out of the conversation. The way I had been before, when they planned how I would get out in the chest.

"Well. We don't have to decide right now," Shahrazad said. "Come back tomorrow morning, and we'll talk again. And, Marjan—don't tell *anyone!*"

Soon after I left, I heard footfalls behind me again. When I turned to look, I saw the corner of a green robe vanish behind a tall urn. Soraya.

This was unbearable! I paused for a moment to think.

I could try to lose her. But even if I succeeded, what would I do then? Hide from her all day?

I could try to ignore her, but that would be hard.

I wondered . . . what would she do if I went up on the roof to see Zaynab?

I would find out!

I took a roundabout route to the spiral kitchen stairs, half hoping that Soraya would give up and leave me alone. But she didn't. I could hear a faint swishing behind me, and sometimes the hurried padding of bare feet on tile. When I came out on the roof, I looked back down at the steps. The whole top spiral was empty. But I had a feeling Soraya was lower down, lurking around a bend. Still, she would have nowhere to hide on the roof. She would just have to lurk.

I spent all morning up on the roof terrace with Zaynab.

She showed me how to take care of the pigeons—how to feed them, how to clear a clouded eye or mend a cut foot. She taught me how to act around the pigeons, to acknowledge them with a look when you came near. They expected it of you, she said. It was only polite. She said they could tell what kind of a mood you were in—if you were happy, or sick, or mad. She showed me how to roll up the message paper—tightly!—and how to slip it into the tiny wooden capsule and fasten it to a pigeon's leg. You had to do it just right. Make it not so tight that it would cut off the bird's blood flow, but snug enough so that it wouldn't fall off. Gently, gently, Zaynab said. And afterward, she let me throw one of her birds into the air.

There was something calming about Zaynab, about her pavilion high above the palace, about the burbling of her birds. She had a name for each one, and she treated them with a tenderness that made me think, for some reason, of my mother. Words came easier now between us, and her humming seemed happy—not nervous and strange.

I longed to confide in her, to tell her about the storyteller and my idea about the pigeons. But Shahrazad had told me not to. So I didn't.

We ate after noon prayers—cheese and raisins and fresh bread that Zaynab cooked over a brazier. Several birds still perched on her shoulders, but she didn't have to wash anything this time. There was a stack of clean cups and bowls on a wooden shelf. And the floor had been scrubbed as well.

Just as we were finishing our meal, the young eunuch with the soft face came and summoned Zaynab to Shahrazad.

He must be the one, I thought.

Zaynab said that I could stay, but I didn't. I went down to my room for a nap. I didn't see Soraya. But just before I slipped off to sleep, I thought I heard, outside my room, the clinking of game tiles on the floor.

The next morning, Shahrazad summoned me again, just as she had done the day before. When I entered her chamber, I heard pigeons cooing and, looking about, saw two slender bird baskets in a corner of the room. I could see through the wicker that there were three levels inside, with birds on every one.

Shahrazad told me the new plan. There were still a lot of *ifs*'s and uncertainties to it. The parts that happened inside the harem seemed clear and plausible—at least, the parts that she told me. Someone was helping us, and she wouldn't say who.

But the outside-the-harem parts were full of foggy patches and outright mistakes. "A thousand pardons," I said. "There are *many* carpet merchants in the bazaar. We'll need to know which one." And, "The merchants don't transport oil in ceramic jars. They use leather ones, because they're lighter." I told Shahrazad that silver dirhams and copper fils were better than gold dinars— less conspicuous. I asked for veils that were not so fine. "And Dunyazad needs to take off her rings. All of them. We want her to look poor." But I could still wear my silver-and-garnet comb, I told myself, because it would be covered.

All the while, I felt a growing uneasiness. Shahrazad and her sister were as naive about the outer world as I was about the harem. They had no grasp of it at all!

Still, this plan—once I had helped them press the wrinkles out of it—seemed as if it might work.

If we were lucky.

I returned to the roof.

This day, I found Zaynab preparing to lower a lidded basketful of pigeons over the side. "The pigeon boy is waiting," she said.

"What will he do with them?"

"He'll give them to a caravan master, who will take them far across the kingdom so that people can send back messages to the Sultan."

Near the edge of the roof was a sort of barrel on its side, with rope wrapped around it. You could turn it with a handle, like a spit. A winch, Zaynab called it. There was a hook on the end of the rope, which Zaynab attached to a ring at the top of the basket. I pulled my veil over my head and peered down as Zaynab turned the winch and the basket descended with a loud creaking noise. The boy was standing on the street, looking up. I watched him slip the hook off the ring and then scamper away, the basket dangling from his hand.

I stayed there all day, on the roof with Zaynab and her birds. I loved holding the pigeons' soft bodies against mine, taking off the treasured messages and putting them in the small silver casket, which Zaynab delivered to the Sultan's guards. I loved the dusty smell of feathers and the birds' burbling coos when I stroked their heads. I began to get to know them by the names Zaynab had given them, began to tell them apart by the colors of their feathers and by how they behaved. Twice, I caught myself talking to them and, once, a pigeon flew up onto my shoulder and pecked at my hair.

As I looked out across the city to the green hills at the horizon, my mind started to open up and think about things I had locked out in my fever to get the stories. What lay beyond those hills? I wondered. What kind of places had all those women and girls gone to when they escaped from the city? In the tales, the world beyond the green hills was filled with wonders—carved wooden horses that fly, islands where the soil is made of diamonds, vast kingdoms ruled by women.

Zaynab and I lay on our backs at sunset, watching the pink and purple clouds go sailing across the sky. Then, after prayers, I asked how she had come to live here. She told me that her grandfather had been governor of the messenger pigeons many years ago and that her mother, a wily woman, had finagled the position for her. "I worked for the old sultan, Shahryar's father," she said. "The old one promised my mother never to replace me—but his son tried to once." She laughed softly.

"What's funny?" I asked.

"He put in a man who didn't know a pigeon from a duck. He made a mess of things, and so Shahryar called me back."

"Were you here when . . . during the purge?"

Zaynab nodded, suddenly grave. "I used to . . . go down to the harem sometimes. I had friends there. But after the . . . Well, now I don't go there anymore. It was terrible. It—" She turned away from me; I lay still and listened to the deep, mournful cooing of the birds. In a moment, Zaynab turned back and sighed. "I don't . . . get many visitors these days," she said.

The stars came glimmering out in the deep blue dusk, and after a while, I told Zaynab about Auntie Chava and Uncle Eli. A wave of homesickness engulfed me.

And, after a longer while, Zaynab asked me gently about my foot.

I had never told anyone about it. At my old home, where I had lived with my mother, everybody knew. Auntie Chava knew, too, though she never said a word about it. But she would purse her lips and shake her head sometimes, watching me limp. She was angry about it, I could tell.

But I had never told anyone, myself. I never thought I would. Still, lying on the roof beside Zaynab, looking up at the stars . . . she made me feel that it would be all right to tell.

My mother is calling me.

"Marjan. Come here," she says.

I'm afraid. Her voice sounds funny, a little quavery and weak. Her room is dark.

"Come here, Marjan. Come sit beside me."

I tiptoe into the room. I can see her now, in the dimness— her long, pale face, her dark eyes. I sit down beside her on the pallet. She smiles, runs her hand through my hair. She moves her fingers lightly across my forehead, my eyebrows, my cheeks. "Marjan," she says, and I can feel the old warmth now, behind the new strange thinness of her voice. I lean against her; her arms fold me in; I can hear the beating of her heart.

"Marjan," she says again.

She draws in breath and sniffles; I pull away, look into her face. Tears. Her eyes are shining, and there are tears running down her cheeks.

"You'll be all right when I'm gone, my beloved. I know you will. You're strong and you're bright. You're a jewel, Marjan. Always remember that. A beautiful jewel."

Gone? The fear flares up again. "Where are you going?" I ask. "Take me with you. I want to come, too."

She folds me in again, and I feel something trembly in her breath. And then she's moving my foot, pulling it away from my body, twisting it so that one side of it is flat against the floor.

"Hold it just like that," she says, and her voice is so hoarse, it's almost a whisper. "Just for a moment."

I pull my foot away. "Why?" I ask. "I don't want to."

She puts my foot back the way it was. "Just trust me, Marjan," she says. "Leave it there. Just for a moment."

She's moving now, pushing aside her cushion. There's something in her hands, something heavy, something she can barely lift.

"Madar . . ."

"Put your foot back the way I showed you." Her voice is harder now, harder than before.

I put my foot back. She's standing now, holding the thing in her hands. A pot. A heavy pot. It's high in the air now, and she's shaking, but the pot keeps going higher.

"Just for a moment," she says, and then the pot moves and Madar moves and pebbles are flying everywhere and pain explodes in my foot. Someone is screaming, and there are footsteps and loud voices, and the voice is still screaming and the pain is still exploding, and it's bright. It's bright. So bright.

"She did it out of love. You understand that, Marjan, don't you? She did it out of love."

I didn't know how I had gotten there, with Zaynab's

arms around me. I drew in a shaky breath, fought to keep myself from crying. Another breath. I pulled away, let the old familiar anger fend off tears.

"How could a person love you and then hurt you that way?" I demanded. "Maim you for the rest of your life? So that people would laugh at you and nobody would ever marry you and you would always have to be someone else's servant?"

"Marjan! She did it to keep you from the Sultan. He was killing a wife every night. He vowed to keep it up forever. And you were her beautiful little girl, and she wasn't going to be there to protect you."

I knew she did it to protect me. I knew that. But if she had been strong, she would have found another way. If she had been clever and brave, like Shahrazad. If she hadn't given up. Many mothers sent their daughters away over the green hills with Abu Muslem. Many mothers escaped and took their daughters with them. But my mother maimed me, and then drank poison and died.

I knew she did it to protect me. But I would never forgive her for it. I couldn't.

"She should have been strong," I said, and I could hear the coldness in my voice.

Zaynab was shaking her head. Tears were streaming down her face. "This is hard, my dear," she said. "This is very, very hard."

Chapter 14
The Oil Jar

I slept uneasily that night, jolted awake by the slightest sounds: whispers of footsteps outside my door, hushed voices, a child's cry from some far-off corner of the harem. And then came a soft knocking, which at first seemed part of a dream, but was still there when the dream had melted away.

Footsteps, fading to silence.

I rolled up my pallet and groped through darkness toward the doorway, until my foot kicked something soft and lumpy. I leaned down, touched it, ran it through my hands to feel the shape of it. A coarse veil. Good.

I dressed then, by *feel*, except for my sandals, which I held because they would make too much noise. Pulling aside the curtain, I had just enough light to see the shape of a sleeping woman on the floor.

Not sleeping. Drugged. Someone—maybe the one who had knocked—had given her sharbat laced with a sleeping potion. That had been part of the plan.

I bent down, peered into her face. Soraya.

I stole down the stairs and into the courtyard below.

The harem was dark, lit only by a milky moonlight glow that seeped in through the window grills. Shapes loomed before me, just thickenings in the gloom until, as I came near, they sharpened into familiar things: a pillar, a fountain, an urn.

I had memorized the way. Through the courtyard with the blue fountain, down a flight of stairs, through the corridor with the black-and-white-tiled floor, up again to the courtyard with the gold-inlaid ceiling. Then more corridors and more stairs—going down and down and down until I was blind with darkness, but my nose pricked to life with the smell of kitchen spices. Turn right through a narrow doorway; feel for the flint on the table, feel for the lamp.

Light bloomed up before me, illuminating the place where I stood. A storeroom. Crates and baskets and bulging burlap bags were stacked against three walls. A row of huge ceramic jars stood along the fourth—with three tall leather olive oil jars at one end. Two, I saw, had been marked with white chalk.

I had heard, in the old tales, of people hiding inside empty olive oil jars. But the tales never said how they did it. I took off my veil and then, as quietly as I could, dragged some crates in front of one of the marked jars. I stacked them up like stairs, until the highest one came nearly to the lip of the jar. I put on my sandals, then set my veil and the lamp on the uppermost crate. Looking down, I could see that the seam in the leather jar had been taken apart at the top, so I could slip easily through the neck.

I sat on the crate, dangled my feet into the jar. Once in, I wouldn't be able to get back out. Not without help. I took a deep breath, blew out the lamp, then slid down inside the jar. My hips caught, but I pulled at the loosened seam and wriggled through.

It was slick and oily and reeked of olives. When I stood up straight, the top of my head—to my eyes—poked through the neck of the jar. Later, I would have to crouch. I reached one arm up through the opening and, finding my veil, pulled it down through the hole and wrapped it around me.

I stood waiting in the dark.

The bad thing about waiting is that your mind has nothing to do. So then it thinks of things to do—to terrify you. My mind kept sending me pictures of the Khatun, and then the fear would come welling up inside me, and it would be hard to breathe.

What if somebody came into the storeroom with a lamp and saw the stacked crates? What if they found me, and then told the Khatun?

I gave myself something else to think about. The plan, what we had to do.

Ayaz. He was supposed to look for me twice a day at the fountain in the carpet bazaar. And I was sure that he would—because of the dinars. He was probably *living* there now, searching for me, dreaming his greedy little dreams. I went over what I would say to him and to the storyteller.

After a while, my shoulder began to itch. Then my bad foot began to throb, and my leg was cramping up. I had just started to stretch, to push one arm up through the neck of the jar, when I heard the call to morning prayer. I couldn't pray properly in this jar. Later, I would make it up.

Now was the dangerous time. People would be stirring. They might finish their prayers before Dunyazad came.

Soon, I heard the pad of bare footsteps, coming near. Was it Dunyazad? I crouched down into the jar and, looking up, saw light flickering across the ceiling.

They were in here now, the footsteps. I heard a gritty, scraping sound. Someone was moving the crates, scooting them across the floor. It must be Dunyazad!

"Dunyazad?" I said softly.

The scraping sound stopped. Quiet. *Please be Dunyazad,* I thought. The scrapes started up again.

Cold fear gathered around my heart. Why didn't she say something? Why didn't she answer?

Suddenly, a second, lighter set of footsteps, coming fast. The heavier footsteps thudded twice, then were silent. A swish of fabric, a murmur, and then, "Marjan!" came a whispered voice. "Stay down. Take this."

Dunyazad!

Something flat and round appeared above the hole, blocking the flickering light. The bottom of a wicker bird basket. I squatted down as far as I could, guided the basket through the neck of the jar and into the widest part.

Please don't coo, I thought. I breathed in the dusty scent of feathers, mingled with the smell of olive oil. I could feel something moving, could hear the pigeons' feet making scratchy noises. But no cooing.

More thumps and footsteps and scraping noises. Then a huff of breath; the flickering light went black. There came the faintest rustle of fabric, then the retreating *pad pad padding* of the first, heavy footsteps again.

And now the harem was coming to life. I heard women's voices, a shuffling of many slippered footfalls, a feverish din of clangs and bumps and scrapings. My legs had begun to ache from crouching, but I didn't dare stand. I found that if I set my body in a certain way, I could wedge myself into the contours of the jar, with my shins resting against one part of it and my seat against another and the bird basket hugged to my breast.

I waited for the call to withdraw, which would tell the women to leave when the merchant's men came to deliver the oil. And *waited.* I began to think that Dunyazad was wrong—that the oil merchant wouldn't come today, that we would be trapped in these jars until nightfall.

Suddenly, "Withdraw!" I heard. The high, reedy voice of a eunuch. "Withdraw! Withdraw!" There was a flurry of pattering footfalls, and then silence.

Male voices. I could hear them now in the distance—and the clatter of mules' hooves. Heavy, boot-shod footsteps coming near. Something scraped against my jar and then I heard—I almost *felt*—the sound of a body pressed against the jar.

An exhaled breath, just above me. My scalp prickled. I kept my head bowed, but whoever it was could look straight down at my veil. The jar heaved up. I was moving. I braced myself, holding my veil with one hand and the bird basket with the other, pressing my legs and back against the jar.

I couldn't help . . . picturing . . . who it was that carried the jar. He must be strong. I imagined the young eunuch, the one who had smiled at me. He didn't falter, but carried me smoothly outside—I knew it was outside from the brightness that cast shadows into the jar and warmed the top of my head.

My jar lurched suddenly upward, and one of the pigeons let out a sharp *coo*. I held my breath. Had anyone heard?

A creaking sound. The leather straps of the jar harness? Shahrazad had told me that Dunyazad and I would be carried on either side of the same mule in the oil merchant's caravan.

A shout—some distance away. Then more creakings and the hollow clop of hooves on pavement. Now I was moving again, swaying gently. I heard the rhythmic swish of the jar rubbing against the side of the mule.

I ventured a look up; the circle of pale early morning sky joggled above. I could see pieces of buildings, but I couldn't tell which ones they were. A pigeon flew overhead, then a shoulder swam into view, the back of someone's head. I ducked down again.

After a time, we stopped. The mules stomped and blew; their harnesses creaked. Now, footfalls. Voices.

"Wait. I'll get these!" The voice was so near, it startled me. It was deep—not a eunuch's voice. "My nephew needs two leather jars. Keep them on the mule, and I'll have Majeed drive them over."

We began moving again. When we stopped this time,

I peered up through the hole and saw a rough wattle roof. The scents of fur and hay and manure drifted into the jar, overpowering the oil smell and the bird smell.

Footfalls. I ducked my head. Creaking noises. All at once the jar plunged downward, and now I felt firm ground beneath my feet. Not for long. The jar was laid gently on its side; the pigeons cooed, flapping and scrabbling about. I wound up on my back with the pigeon basket above me.

Then a man's voice, near and quiet and low. "Wait. Don't come out now. I don't want to see you. Count to ten slowly, then leave by the stable yard door."

Chapter 15

Just a Friend

"What is that terrible *stench*?"

Dunyazad brushed hay off her clothes while I finished wriggling out of my jar.

I didn't smell any stench. Just ordinary stable smells and a hint of the street.

"Hurry, Marjan! Come *along!*"

I put on my veil and then, with my free hand, righted my bird basket, which I had pushed out of the jar before me. The pigeons fluttered and cooed indignantly. "Are you all right, little birds?" I asked softly. I peered inside; none seemed to be injured. So I snatched up the basket by the ring at the top and followed Dunyazad across the barnyard. She was already fumbling with the latch on the heavy wooden gate. She pulled the gate open, picked up her basket, stepped outside—then stopped.

"What's the matter?" I asked. I looked beyond her into a stream of people and animals: a ragged goat boy and his bleating flock, two men on camels, a fisherman lugging two sloshing pails, a carter, a woman with a stack of flatbread balanced on her head, a band of shouting street urchins pestering a man toting a basketful of oranges. The smells and the din, muted in the courtyard, now clashed in my nose and ears.

"What's the matter?" I asked again, but Dunyazad only stared. "Look out!" I grabbed Dunyazad's elbow and yanked her back out of the path of a donkey cart. The driver lurched to one side, cursing at her. She cried out sharply, her eyes snapping with anger. "How *dare* he!" she said. "How *dare* he!"

"Dunyazad—stop!" I said. Quickly I straightened my veil, which had slipped when I let go to grab her. Now I felt like shaking her. I would have, too, if she hadn't been bigger than me . . . and a princess. "What's the matter?" I asked for the third time. Then all at once I knew. She'd never been out of the harem. She'd never smelled air that wasn't perfumed. She'd never been around so many people all at once.

Dunyazad peered out at the street again. "Where do we

go now?" She sounded uncertain—so unlike her usual self.

"This way," I said. "To the fountain to wait for Ayaz." I led her into the street, merging into the flow of people moving toward the bazaar. I wished I had a free hand to pull her along behind me, as she had done in the dark passageways in the harem. I kept looking back, calling out things for her to watch out for—a cart coming from behind, a pile of dung, an overloaded porter cutting across the current.

"Are we almost there?" she asked.

"Do you see those domed roofs? That's the bazaar!"

We came in at the portal by the brass bazaar, then wove through it to the mahogany bazaar, then the cotton sellers' bazaar. Often, I had to wait for Dunyazad, who gaped like a visitor from another world. When I began to feel impatient, I reminded myself that this *was* another world—to her. Once, I had to stop her from giving a gold dinar to a skin-and-bones beggar boy with flies buzzing around his eyes. "But he's *hungry!*" she said.

"If you give that to him, we'll have every beggar in the bazaar swarming around us and we'll never get the rest of the tale."

She put the coin away. "I just want to feed him," she said. "What will he do if no one feeds him?"

I handed the boy a copper fils, thinking, same as they all do. Same as they've done forever. Same as they would always do, unless the sultans and rich people opened their coffers. And there was little chance of that.

At last we came to the fountain. The man with the trained monkey was there again. I looked about for Ayaz, but he was nowhere to be found. "Now we wait," I told Dunyazad.

"Are you certain he'll come?"

I nodded, trying to seem sure of myself. Of course he would! I'd seen his eyes when he looked at those dinars.

Dunyazad drew forward, watching the monkey perform. I stayed back a little way, so I could look over the crowd in the bazaar. I saw a boy walking by with a drum, and another lugging a bulging burlap sack for an old woman. I saw a boy climbing up a huge pile of folded carpets, as if he were scaling a mountain. A merchant pointed and yelled at him. The boy tugged at a carpet in the pile until it came loose, then tossed it down to the man.

No Ayaz.

After a while, the man with the trained monkey picked up his bowlful of coins, signaled for the monkey to leap onto his shoulder, and left.

Dunyazad looked at me. She didn't say anything. She didn't have to. *Where was Ayaz?*

What if he had come already, before we had arrived? What if he didn't come again until late afternoon? That would ruin our plans. That would be *dangerous*, because the Khatun would discover that we'd gone.

"Sister?"

I turned around and there was Ayaz, grinning his impish grin. "Who is your friend?" he asked.

"You don't need to know," I said quickly, trying to stop Dunyazad from blurting out her name. "Just take us to the storyteller."

"What are the birds for?" Ayaz asked, not moving.

I had a terrible thought, then. *Pigeon pie.*

"Not for *you*," I said crossly. "Let's go."

Ayaz held out his hand, still grinning.

I sighed. "We've been through this before! I'll pay you when we get there. Four copper fils."

He looked hurt. "Have I displeased you so much, Lady, that you would cut my wage from gold to copper?"

"I didn't have the right change before. Now I do."

"But now there are two of you. It's twice as much work. So my fee has gone up to two gold dinars."

"*Two gold dinars?*" I whispered, furious. "I'll find him myself, then."

He shrugged. "You're welcome to try. But if she—" he nodded at Dunyazad—"is as fine a lady as my nose tells me she is, you're lucky I'm not charging you three."

Perfume. Dunyazad was wearing perfume! *Expensive* perfume. I could smell it now—that smell like rain— though I hadn't noticed it before.

"Two silver dirhams, when we get there. That's my last offer."

He shook his head. "Gold," he said. "Two of them."

And then, so quickly I didn't have time to stop her, Dunyazad set down her birds, plucked two dinars from her sash, and handed them to Ayaz. "Thank you, gracious lady!" he said. He grinned at me, then whirled round and dived into the crowd.

I set off—running—after him, my pigeon basket bumping against my legs. "You shouldn't have done that!" I said over my shoulder to Dunyazad. "Now he's probably gone for good!" I didn't care if she *was* a princess. She had ruined everything!

"Two dinars is nothing," she said, close behind me. "We don't have time to haggle."

"You might as well come right out and tell him who you are, then," I said. "*Nobody* can afford to pay that much. And even if they could, they *wouldn't*. And now that he's got what he wants from us, he'll just leave!"

Ayaz was far ahead now, weaving in and out among porters and mule drivers and shoppers. Soon he vanished altogether.

"He's . . . gone!" Dunyazad said, and now she sounded sorry.

We stood there in the street while people flowed around us. I searched for Ayaz, avoiding Dunyazad's eyes. Then, "Look, Marjan! There he is!" She pointed up a small flight of stairs, beneath a carved stone arch. He was motioning us to come.

It seemed longer this time until we came to the place where he had blindfolded me before. The pigeons grew heavier with every step. Ayaz disappeared and returned with two kerchiefs, apologizing profusely to Dunyazad for having to blindfold her. He had never apologized to *me*, I thought bitterly. Dunyazad looked worried, but I reassured her. "He did this before," I said. "Remember, I told you?" Still, it was scary. If anyone found out who she was . . . More than ever, I questioned the wisdom of having her along.

"Lady, you hold on to her veil," Ayaz told Dunyazad, nodding at me. "I'll carry your basket, so you'll have a hand free."

"*I* won't have a hand free," I said.

"I'll guide you like this." Ayaz hooked one finger through the ring at the top of my pigeon basket.

Dunyazad held my veil as Ayaz blindfolded us. Then he led us to the storyteller's house. Inside, I set down my pigeons and pulled off the kerchief.

"You brought a friend," the storyteller said.

I looked at Dunyazad. Ayaz had removed her blind-fold, but she kept her veil taut about the moon of her face and her eyes turned down toward the carpet. For once, she was silent.

The storyteller raised his shaggy brows, waiting, I thought, for me to introduce her. I didn't. "And you brought pigeons," he said at last.

"You said the story was long. And we have to leave before noon. The pigeons are trained to return . . . to where we live. You can send whatever's left of the story with them. If you can't write, we'll give you coins to pay a scribe."

"So they're Zaynab's birds," he said. It stopped me cold.

He was far ahead of me. I had so carefully not told him anything about us—who we were and where we had come from—yet he knew, somehow, that we had come from the harem. And he knew of Zaynab. How did he know of Zaynab? *I* had never heard of Zaynab until a week ago.

I had the feeling again that he was something other than what he seemed—and that it went far beyond the fact that he could see while he had pretended to be blind.

"Who are you?" I asked. "How do you know of Zaynab?"

"We'll trade," he said. "I'll tell you who I am if you'll tell me who your friend is."

"She's just a *friend*," I said.

Long silence. At last the storyteller said, "Well. Then I'll tell you more of the story; you have a little time. Sit down before me and listen."

Chapter 16

No Way In

The storyteller told how Badar Basim was swept by the sea onto a bewitched land, where he met a grocer who wasn't really a grocer, but a magician in disguise. Meanwhile, Badar Basim fell into the clutches of the evil

Queen Lab. She turned him into a Stinking Bird and put him in a cage and denied him food and water.

Then it was time for us to go.

Though the tale kept me interested the whole time, some parts of it made me uneasy. The Sultan already had a bad enough opinion of women without making it worse by telling about Queen Lab. And, while I understood what Shahrazad had said, that you have to have all kinds of women in your tales, it didn't seem wise to ask for trouble by telling about a woman who was evil through and through.

But there was no help for it. This was the tale the Sultan wanted, so this was what Shahrazad would have to tell.

While Ayaz was tying Dunyazad's blindfold, I turned to the storyteller. "You *will* send the birds with the rest of the tale, won't you? Send them *soon*? Be sure to use thin paper, and write small. I can show you how to tie on a message—"

"Don't worry, Little Pigeon." His voice was gentle, warm, the way it sometimes sounded in his story. Though he didn't smile, his eyes crinkled at their edges, as if I had amused him. "Go along home, now. You can rely on me."

I felt better then. A little. But I still didn't like leaving so much to trust and hope. While Ayaz blindfolded me, I pretended to scratch the bridge of my nose and pushed up the kerchief until I could see a little bit—the floor and the bottoms of walls. I hoped never to come to this place again. And yet, if the pigeons never arrived . . . It would be best to be able to find the storyteller again.

Ayaz took me by the elbow, and Dunyazad gripped my free hand. Looking down beneath the blindfold, I saw

140

the bottom of a rough wooden door. Down three stone steps, turn right along a blackened mud wall, turn left, turn right and then right again, turn left to walk along a wall with three branching cracks in a row. Ayaz took off our blindfolds at the same place as before, then led us back to the fountain. He stood there a moment, waiting. I thought he wanted more money and was about to argue, but then he nodded and said, "I take my leave of you, Ladies. Allah grant you good fortune."

We watched until he was out of sight, then went searching for the stall of the carpet merchant Shahrazad had told us about. It was not far from the fountain, she had said. The merchant would be sitting in front, on a scarlet-and-blue carpet, and wearing an orange turban with a purple feather. We were to approach him and say, "We're here for the small round carpets."

We found him right away—a skinny man with a scraggly beard. No sooner had I opened my mouth and said, "We're here for—" than he leaped to his feet and, motioning us to follow, led us around a corner and into a narrow alley to a cart that was harnessed to a mule. The man jabbed a finger at the cart. "Get in," he said. Then he squeezed himself through the gap between the cart and a wall, turned a corner, and was gone.

I looked about me. Ahead, where the alley met with the street, the sun streamed down, lighting up a moving stream of people. Behind, the alley made a sharp bend, and I couldn't see beyond it. From the bend to the street, the alley was deserted. Except for the mule—and us.

The cart's back gate hung open; two loosely rolled carpets lay within. Dunyazad glanced at me, took a deep breath and, pushing with her feet, burrowed into one of the carpets up to her waist. But now she was having trouble. She kicked at the air; I heard little sighs and *oofs*. I grasped her ankles and pushed. She scooted forward, all the way into the carpet, until I really had to *look* to see her feet.

My turn now. And no one to help. I scrunched my shoulders together, pushed myself into the dark tunnel of carpet. It was a tight fit. Dust filled my nose; I wanted to sneeze. Weren't these carpets supposed to have been cleaned? Lying on my forearms with the carpet pressing against the back of my head and shoulders and back, I shoved off with my feet and squirmed forward on my elbows, wriggling like a worm. The carpet grabbed at me, pulled my veil back. My head was bare now, and everything below my waist was poking out behind. Then . . . footsteps. Someone took hold of my ankles; I shot forward, then abruptly stopped.

Moving my feet, I could tell that they were surrounded by carpet.

Now the cart gate creaked and thudded behind me. A sudden lurch: we were moving. Rumbling filled my ears, filled my body. I took shallow breaths of the dusty air—through my mouth, so I wouldn't sneeze. Sweat trickled down into the outer corners of my eyes, but my hands were pinned beneath me and I couldn't reach to wipe it away.

This was worse than the chest and the jar. Much worse.

At last the cart halted. I heard voices nearby. They grew louder. Arguing. I couldn't make out all of the words. But I thought I heard the higher voices saying, "Unroll them," and the low voice kept saying *no*.

Something was wrong.

The air in the carpet grew hotter, thicker, dustier. I couldn't bear it much longer. Sweat poured off my body; my eyes stung with it. My forearms and hands were going numb. I wanted to thrash about, push my way out to fresh air. A sudden *thud*. The cart was moving again—fast—squeaking, rattling, jolting. What had happened?

And now, beyond the muffled street sounds, I heard the call of a moazzen for noon prayers. I felt terrible, missing prayers for the second time.

The cart jerked to a halt. Footfalls, coming round behind. The creak of the back gate. Then a voice, a loud whisper: "Get out!"

This was not right. We were supposed to be taken to Shahrazad and only come out when she said to.

"Get *out* of my cart, I tell you! Are you deaf! They won't let the carpets into the harem!"

Then footfalls, running, growing fainter.

I lay there sucking in the dusty, suffocating air, not knowing what to do. My clothes were damp and clung to me; I lay in a pool of my own sweat. More than anything, I wanted to get *out* of this stifling carpet!

But was it safe?

Quiet. The city sounds had stilled, except for the distant rumbling voices of men at prayer.

I began to scoot backward. The carpet shoved my clothes forward as I moved, until everything but my under trousers was clumped in a damp wad about my head. I prayed there was no one there to see. But I had to get out. With all the cloth around my face, I could hardly breathe. At last I could bend at my hips; my feet hit ground. I backed all the way out, then pulled my gown and robes and veil from the carpet roll and hastily rearranged everything until I was decently covered.

The cart stood in a deserted alley—a different alley from before. The mule turned, looked at me, then snorted and stomped its foot.

The driver was nowhere in sight.

"Lady?" I said. I peered through the tunnel of Dunyazad's carpet at the bottoms of her sandals. "I think you'd better get out. There's no one here."

The carpet thrashed around, but the sandals didn't come any nearer. Then a muffled voice. It sounded like, "I can't!"

Dunyazad wasn't as skinny as me. I took hold of her ankles and pulled. When she was out to her waist, I stopped pulling and turned away to let her compose herself. Rustling sounds. Then, "What are we doing here? Why aren't we home? Where is the driver?" She sounded irritated, demanding, the way she sometimes did in the harem.

"I don't know," I said. "Did you hear that argument? With the palace guards? I think they wanted to unroll the carpets and the driver got scared."

"But he can't just *leave* us here," Dunyazad said. "He wouldn't dare!"

I didn't say anything. He clearly *could* leave us here. He clearly *had* dared.

"What are we going to do now?" she asked, and I thought I heard the tiniest bit of a whine.

I swallowed. She was afraid. Brave Dunyazad was afraid. *I* was afraid, too. But . . . She was counting on me now. I was *responsible* for her.

We couldn't just walk up to the palace guards and ask

144

them to let us back in. If it were only a matter of a lashing, I would do it. I would tell Dunyazad to do it. But . . . sneaking out of the Sultan's harem, without permission . . . He'd probably have us killed.

"What about the friend . . . who helped us get out?" I asked. "Couldn't that person—whoever it is—couldn't that person help?"

"No! The Khatun would . . . No. Anyway, how could we reach . . . that person . . . without getting caught ourselves?"

I didn't know.

"Shahrazad . . ." Her voice broke; she turned away from me.

This was bad, very bad. Though the Khatun always slept late, she would be up by now. She'd know that I'd slipped away from Soraya; they were probably searching for me. Maybe it would take longer for them to miss Dunyazad. She often disappeared into the long passageways for hours and nobody thought anything of it. But if she didn't return for the story tonight . . .

What could we do? Marjan, *think!*

A flapping of wings: a pigeon flew overhead. Then it came to me. A message! We could send a message to Zaynab—a message for Shahrazad.

We set off for the storyteller's house. The crowd had thinned in the midday heat; soon, I knew, the streets would be nearly deserted. I found my way to the fountain and from there tried to retrace our route. We passed by the carved stone arch where we had waited for Ayaz. We went down a flight of seven steps followed by a flight of five. I remembered that. We lost our way once, so we doubled back and tried one street after another until we happened upon one that looked familiar. Finally, we reached the last poor street, the one where Ayaz had blindfolded us. Before he had taken off my blindfold, I had seen, peering down, the bottom of a mud wall with three branching cracks in a row. And there *were* three branching cracks a little way down an alley. I moved in that direction. "Are you certain you know the right way?" Dunyazad asked. "You truly could see?"

"A little," I said.

The alley was narrow and dingy. I turned right, then left twice, and then forgot which way I was supposed to go until I saw, ahead, the alley with the blackened wall. Three stone steps had led up to the gate. "This way!" I said. But *all* the gates—four of them—had three stone steps in front. I stopped, not knowing which door to knock on, not certain at all that this was the right place.

Suddenly, one of the doors flew open and a boy came out, ran away from us down the alley. "Ayaz!" I called.

He stopped, whirled round, gaped at us. "How did you get here?" he demanded. "You're supposed to be back with her sister! With . . . Shahrazad!"

Chapter 17
Like Princess Budur

LESSONS FOR LIFE AND STORYTELLING

The tale of Princess Budur isn't the only one where women dress up as men and nobody knows the difference. This happens a lot in the old stories. Sometimes women disguised as men even rule entire countries and do a good job.

Dunyazad was right about Princess Budur—and all the rest of those story women who dress up as men and do man things perfectly well. One thing those tales are saying underneath is that women aren't inferior. They're equal to men.

Still, there's more to disguise than changing your clothes. The best disguise can be just a *look*.

I caught my breath. It was one thing for Ayaz to know that we were from the Sultan's harem—but quite another for him to know that Shahrazad's very own sister was standing before him in the alley.

"Come in! Quickly! *Come!*" The storyteller stood inside the gate, motioning furiously.

We hurried across the courtyard and into the house. The storyteller fixed Ayaz with his keen gaze. "Did anyone hear them? Did anyone see?"

"No, Aga," Ayaz said. "There was no one in the alley."

"You need to be *discreet*, Ayaz! You need to watch your tongue! And—" He glanced at me and Dunyazad; I caught that crinkle at the edges of his eyes. "When you lead a blindfolded person, make sure she isn't peeking!"

Ayaz looked down at the floor. "Yes, Aga. I'm sorry."

Now the storyteller's eyes turned grave. "Could anyone have followed you?" he asked me.

"I . . . I don't know," I said, feeling foolish. I hadn't thought to look.

The storyteller said something in a low voice to Ayaz; the boy slipped out the front door. "We'll try to get you back in the harem," the storyteller said, "but I don't know if we can do it today. You may have to spend the night—"

"We can't!" Dunyazad said. "Or *I* can't. I'm—"

"Your . . . sister would miss you?"

Dunyazad looked at me; I nodded. Our secret was out. No use trying to hide it. The storyteller had tossed out his guess about Zaynab, and we had confirmed it, and he had surmised the rest. We *had* to trust him now.

"She still keeps up the pretense that the stories are for me," Dunyazad told him. "Without the pretense . . . I don't know what the Sultan would do."

The storyteller didn't seem surprised. "Very well, then," he said grimly. "We'll get you back by tonight. One way or another."

Tonight? My insides went liquid with fear. What about the Khatun? The longer we were gone, the more certain she was to miss me. And last time, she had been *furious*. What she would do if she caught me out again . . .

"It would be best to return *before* tonight," I said. "We could send one of Zaynab's birds—"

"And how would that work, Little Pigeon? Shahrazad would have to send someone to fetch you here, or you'd have to wait someplace else for them to fetch you. And then . . . Does she have another way of smuggling you into the harem? Or are enough of the palace guards your . . . friends?"

I didn't know. I turned to Dunyazad. She shook her head.

The storyteller looked thoughtful. "Well," he said, "then we'll have to do something else. When Ayaz returns, we'll know how things stand."

He had an air of confidence that gave me hope. And yet it frightened me to think how much he knew. *Everything*. And we knew nothing about him. I wondered again who he was, and why he knew this story that only the Sultan seemed to have heard. I suddenly thought of that grocer, that grocer in the tale who wasn't really a grocer but a magician in disguise.

"Since you left, I've sent seven birds with bits of the story to Zaynab," the storyteller said now. "I was about to send the eighth when you came. But perhaps I should tell as much as I can to the both of you, in case something should happen to the pigeons."

Something happen to the pigeons? There was another morsel to add to my soup of worries!

As the story unwound, I saw what Shahrazad had been saying about things balancing out. The evil Queen Lab and her scheming mother were balanced by Julnar and *her* mother, who were strong and intelligent and kind. And also there was Marsinah, the slave girl who took pity on Badar Basim. Finally, at the very end, Badir Basim forgave Princess Jauharah. After all she had done to him—changing him into a bird and banishing him to an island with no water and nothing to eat. But he still loved her. Though they brought all the beautiful girls in the kingdom for him to choose from, he wanted only her.

"And when Princess Jauharah's father told her of this," the storyteller said, "these were her words: 'Do as you wish, for sorrow and spite have come to an end, and I agree to be his wife.'"

The storyteller smiled. "We leave them in happiness! May Allah bring the same to you and all who stand in need."

"That's all?" I couldn't help myself; I couldn't believe that was the end.

"The ending displeases you?" he asked.

"He just *forgave* her? After all she did to him? And she wasn't even punished?"

"Oh," the storyteller said. "So you're an advocate of punishment."

"Of *justice!*" I said. "And how could he live, lying beside her at night, knowing how she had deceived him?"

The storyteller looked off into the distance, combing his beard with his fingers. "Well, don't you think it best," he asked at last, "for the Sultan to hear a tale that favors forgiveness?"

Slowly, I nodded. It would be a good lesson for the Sultan, forgiveness. Still, the ending didn't satisfy *me*.

"How did you come by that?" the storyteller abruptly asked, staring at my foot, which poked out beneath my gown.

Hastily, I covered it. "An accident," I said. Suddenly, my face felt hot.

"I heard a story some years ago," he said, "of a woman who had a young daughter and feared for her, so—"

I cut him off. "Don't put me in one of your stories!"

Silence, again. My angry words hung in the air. I saw that Dunyazad was looking at me with startled eyes. At last, the storyteller spoke. "We all have our demons to deal with, Little Pigeon. It's when we cherish them— cradle them to our breasts and feed them day after day— that's when they curdle our souls."

Just after sunset prayers, Ayaz returned. He whispered something into the storyteller's ear and handed him a heap of clothing. The storyteller divided the heap, gave half to Dunyazad and half to me. The cloth was coarse-woven, like Auntie Chava's cloaks. But brightly colored. Garish. With stains, I saw, and patches. I held up the garments one by one to see what they were. A bodyshirt, a cloak, a winding-scarf for a headdress. And not a veil among them. *Boys'* clothes!

"A family of musicians is going into the harem tonight," the storyteller said. "Four brothers and their sons. They have consented to let you go with them and pretend to be part of their family. Once inside, you can break away from the group. Now, go into the next room and change."

"But . . ." I looked at Dunyazad. "I thought they didn't let men into the harem."

"Sometimes they bring in entertainers," she said. "We watch through slits in the curtains, so they can't see us."

"But . . . they'll see *us*," I said. "You and me. Unveiled!"

"It's the only way," the storyteller said. "It'll be dark, and these men can be trusted."

I hesitated.

"Princess Budur did it," Dunyazad said, "and so can we."

It was *not* dark—not quite—though shadows lay thick upon the streets. All the light in the world seemed to have wicked up into the sky, a luminous sapphire blue. A soft breeze cooled the air.

I kept my head down as we followed Ayaz to the musicians' cart. But Dunyazad didn't. She had cast off her unnatural meekness and stood tall again, striding powerfully after Ayaz. At last she was dressed as a boy, like Princess Budur. As we approached the cart, she drew me aside. "Stand up straight, Marjan. You don't *look* like a boy, with your eyes downcast that way."

I didn't feel like a boy. I just felt *strange* in these clothes. They were rough against my skin, after the soft gowns I'd grown used to. Worse, my long braid was knotted up on my head, secured with pins and my garnet comb, and tucked into the headdress. I was afraid my hair would come *un*pinned at any moment and slither down my back. But worst of all by far, I was walking around on the streets with no veil, with the outside air touching my neck and ears. I felt *naked*.

Ayaz nodded good-bye to us, his eyes carefully averted. We climbed up into the cart, setting the burlap-wrapped bundles of our harem clothes in our laps, and sat on the floor among the musicians. One handed Dunyazad a small drum and said to me, "You're a singer." Then he shifted, turned away from us—as all the others had done.

We rode in silence through the narrow alleys and

streets. At last, I saw the bulk of the palace looming before us. Moonlight frosted its domes and silvered the outlines of the trees beyond. We stopped near the southern door. The musicians picked up their instruments and stepped out of the cart. Dunyazad and I followed. *Walk smoothly! Don't limp!* I told myself. It was good that the cloak was overlong and hid all but the toes of my bad foot. Two helmeted palace guards stood on either side of the massive arched door, their hands on the hilts of their scimitars. Most of the musicians went before us, but three of them waited to go behind. I held my breath as Dunyazad neared the guards, moved into the flickering patch of torchlight between them.

Then she was past.

My turn now. *Don't limp.* I looked down, watched my toes. Just as they moved into the light, one of the guards stepped forward, stopped me. "What's in the bundle?" he growled.

My heart was pounding in my throat. "Change of costumes," I said, trying to keep my voice steady, trying to deepen it a little. I remembered to stand tall—like Dunyazad, like Princess Budur. Then, with all the boldness I could muster, I looked straight into the palace guard's eyes. A woman would not do that. No woman would ever do that.

A sudden bright trill sounded behind me. I glanced back. A piper, and now a drummer, were playing. As the guard turned to look, a bell-ringer shooed me quickly past.

I hastened after Dunyazad and the other musicians as they followed a guard through a long colonnaded corridor. He stopped at a wooden door and spoke to a eunuch;

Dunyazad and I huddled in the middle of the group. And then the eunuch was moving through the doorway, calling out, "Withdraw!" We followed him through the empty kitchens, their high, vaulted ceilings blackened with smoke. Dunyazad pulled on my arm, tugging me into an alcove. She pushed on a wooden panel; it opened. She nudged me inside. I stood in the dark, listened to the *click* of a closing door. I heard her beside me, breathing hard. Then her voice, near my ear: "Change into your harem clothes. Leave the other ones here; I'll get rid of them later."

It was black as ebony; impossible to tell what things *were* except by feel. I fumbled about and once tripped on my sash and nearly fell. Nearby, I heard soft grunts and rustlings, then a muttered curse. At last I was dressed—as well as I could manage. I unpinned my hair and tucked in my precious comb.

"Where are you, Marjan? Hold out your hand." Dunyazad patted down my arm to my hand, grasped it, pulled me along behind her. "There's not much time," she said. "Make sure people see you, so they know you're here. I have to get to my sister."

She led me a long way in the dark until at last, we stopped. "Go out here. You'll know the place. I'll see you in the morning."

I did know it: the room where she had taken me into the passage the day I had escaped in the chest. Some way off, I could hear strains of lilting music. Maybe if I just slipped into the crowd watching the musicians, no one would know I'd been gone.

I could *hope*.

Following the sounds, I found a group of women

gathered around a curtained wall that divided a large room in half. They were peering through slits in the brocaded fabric. I crept into the room, stood just behind them. No one turned around. No one had seen.

I let out my breath in a sigh.

"Marjan!"

I spun round. Ashraf! She grabbed my arm, yanked me toward the door. "The Khatun wants to see you," she said.

"*Now.*"

Chapter 18

Prisoner

LESSONS FOR LIFE AND STORYTELLING

Sometimes I wonder if the stories you tell begin to tug at your life, begin to change it in some mysterious way. Not just that you learn from stories, though that can happen, too. But even deeper: Could it be that, by choosing certain stories, you draw to yourself the happenings inside them? So that your life begins to echo your stories?

Ashraf gripped my arm and pulled me down the hallway toward the stairs. I stumbled, lost my footing, but she didn't stop—didn't even slow down. She just kept on dragging me until I was sure my arm was going to wrench out of its socket, until my feet, scrambling around, finally got themselves underneath me again.

My mind froze in terror around the image of the Khatun. I couldn't think. I gave a hard, twisting yank with my arm, slipped out of Ashraf's grasp, and fled away from the stairs. I landed wrong on my bad foot, stumbled, and Ashraf was there again. She grabbed my braided hair and hauled me to the steps, then up. Pain jolted through my neck, burned like fire in my scalp. I tried to keep up with her to ease the fury of the pain, but she was moving fast, moving through courtyards and hallways and up another long flight of steps until at last we came to the Khatun's quarters.

The smell again. The sickly sweet, rotten smell. I couldn't see her, could see nothing but the dark carpets because of the way Ashraf held my braid. As we drew deeper into the dim room, the smell grew stronger, flooded my nose and throat until I was choking with it.

"Here she is," Ashraf said. She flung me to the floor; I hit hard and stayed, my face just inches from the Khatun's feet. Tiny feet—shod in perfect bejeweled slippers, with pouches of fat mounding up around their rims. "I caught her going to see the musicians," Ashraf was saying. "I have no idea where she's been."

"*Get . . . up.*" That voice. That soft, hoarse voice.

I rose slowly, studying the Khatun's face. Though the bloated surface of it seemed calm, I could see something in her eyes, something deep and raging. Behind her, in the shadows, Soraya looked different. There was a soft, wounded look about her. Her eyes were red and puffy, as if she had been crying.

"Where were you?" the Khatun demanded.

"I was—" I started to say *with Zaynab*. But maybe they had searched there. "I was here and there, around the harem."

Her hand whipped out at me before I saw it coming. The slap stung, brought tears to my eyes. I rubbed at my cheek, tried to blink back the tears.

"Don't you *dare* lie to me," she said. "Where were you?"

"I was here," I said. "I was here the whole day."

This time, she hit me with her clenched fist. Pain shot

through my cheek. I staggered backward, caught a foot in the hem of my gown, fell to the floor. She was standing over me now. I scooted back like a crab but bumped into Ashraf's legs.

"Who is he?" the Khatun asked. "Who is she exchanging messages with? When do they meet?"

He? Exchanging messages? A meeting? I struggled to understand but couldn't grasp what she was saying.

"I know she has a lover—she can't hide it from me. They all do. Let them live a month beyond the wedding and they're plotting with their lovers against my son. *Who is he?* Tell me!"

She was talking about Shahrazad. She thought—

"No," I said. "There is no lover! She—"

"Tell me!"

The Khatun's foot thrust out and caught me in the ribs. I rolled onto my stomach, but she kept on kicking—little vicious jabs. My sides were on fire with pain. Somewhere in the back of my mind I wondered how she could keep this up. She was so fat, she could barely *walk*.

At last the kicks stopped. I could hear her wheezing. "Tell me!" she said.

"She . . . doesn't . . . have . . . a . . . lover." It hurt to talk. It hurt to *breathe*.

I felt her moving heavily away. As the smell of her ebbed, I heard her say, "She knows. I'll wring it out of her. Lock her up—for now."

Ashraf took my arm and hauled me to my feet. Pain sliced through the whole middle of me. I groaned, stooped over, clutched at my ribs. My cheek and eye were throbbing. I stole a look back once as we left—a quick one, because the pain struck again, a jagged bolt of it in my side. In the dim light, I saw that the Khatun had seated herself again on her sofa. Behind her, I half expected to see Soraya's familiar smirk.

But no. She wasn't smirking.

Her face was rigid with fear.

It was a small, musty-smelling room she took me to, in an uninhabited part of the harem. By the feeble light of Ashraf's candle, I could see a chamber pot in the corner. Dust, sprinkled with corpses of dead bugs, carpeted the floor. There were no rugs, no cushions, no hangings, no windows. No ornaments of any kind—except for the cobwebs that festooned the shadowy corners of the room. Something scuttled across the floor. Only a beetle—I *hoped*.

Ashraf hesitated in the doorway, then grudgingly set the candle on the floor. The wooden door thumped shut; I heard the grate of a key in the lock and then footsteps moving away.

I squatted down, leaning against a wall, pressing one hand in upon my hurting ribs and another against my hurting cheek and eye. I couldn't cry. I couldn't think. I couldn't sleep. I knew I should be afraid. But I was numb.

Gradually, my mind unfroze, and thoughts began to skitter across the surface of it.

Would they feed me? I wondered. Or would they leave me here to starve? My thoughts took a weird, sideways jag to Badar Basim, how Princess Jauharah had banished him to an island with no food and no water. Someone had saved him, I remembered—Marsinah, the slave girl. But this was real life—not a tale. There would be no Marsinah for me.

At least we'd gotten the story. So for now, Shahrazad

was no worse off than she'd been before I met her. Unless Dunyazad had been caught. But no. She *wouldn't* be caught.

Still, I'd hoped for so much more. To *save* Shahrazad.

But there could be no saving of her. At best, she was doomed to cast about for new tales day after day so she could survive another night. At worst . . .

I had heard tales of torture in the palace. *I'll wring it out of her,* the Khatun had said. Would I break under the pain, tell the Khatun what she wanted to hear? If the pain was bad enough, would I betray Shahrazad to save myself?

Madar!

The word came to me unbidden: a plea. *You should have stayed with me. You should have smuggled us away with Abu Muslem. You smashed my foot, but it didn't do any good. Are you happy now?* Are *you?*

And I could see her face then, in my mind's eye. But she was not happy. She looked down at me, and her eyes were sad.

I sat up, uncertain what had awakened me. Pain jolted through my body—though not quite as bad as before. My eye still throbbed, and I couldn't get it all the way open. Hunger gnawed at my belly. Though the candle still burned, it slumped on the floor, a mere stump. Soon, it would go out.

And then I heard it: a sound. A grating at the door. A key.

I backed into a far corner, avoiding the cobwebs. Slowly, the door swung open.

In the dim yellow glow of the candle, I made out a

pale face and copper-colored hair. Soraya. She put a finger to her lips, motioning me to hush. That was odd, I thought. Who would hear? Why would it matter?

She closed the door behind her and, moving forward, pulled some objects from the folds of her gown and set them down on the floor.

A full waterskin, an embroidered napkin filled with bread and dates, and three more candles.

"Eat quickly!" she said. "No one's supposed to feed you."

Like Marsinah! But I never thought that *Soraya* would help me. Briefly, I wondered if the food were poisoned. Or drugged, as someone had drugged her sharbat. But hunger overcame my doubts. I gobbled the bread and dates, then washed them down with water. Soraya watched, still standing, lifting her skirts a little so as not to soil them on the filthy floor.

When I had finished, I rose, brushed the dust from my gown.

"This was all I could manage for now," Soraya said. "I'll bring you more tomorrow."

"Why? What do you want from me?"

She licked her lips. "I don't want to marry the Sultan. The Khatun . . . she beat me yesterday when she found out you'd escaped."

I remembered how she had looked the day before—as if she had been crying—and felt a sudden twinge of guilt.

"Now she doesn't trust me. She'd trust me even less if I married her son. I don't think she'd trust any woman who married him."

What was it the Khatun had said? *Let them live a*

month beyond the wedding and they're plotting with their lovers against my son.

"I know you're helping Shahrazad," Soraya said. "But I doubt she's taken a lover. I'm not even certain the Khatun truly thinks that—though she *wants* to. It would suit her ends. She's never liked Shahrazad."

"There is no lover," I said. "But . . . is Shahrazad all right? Has the Khatun . . . done anything to her?"

Soraya shook her head. "No. Not yet."

Then Dunyazad must have returned safely.

"I want to help you help Shahrazad," Soraya said. "I want her to live."

How can I believe you? I thought.

I looked at her—hard—and saw fear. She had changed.

"You have to tell me what you're doing," she said. "So I can help."

I shook my head. "No. I can't tell."

"Then tell me what I can do. To help her stay alive."

I pulled my silver-and-garnet comb out of my hair. Slowly, I held it out. "Here," I said. "Give this to Dunyazad. I'm sure she'll recognize it. Tell her where I am, and why. She deserves to know that. Tell her . . . not to do anything to put herself or her sister in danger for my sake. But tell her that I'm afraid . . . of what they might make me say. What *lies*," I said. "If they hurt me."

Soraya held up the comb to the light. Auntie Chava's comb. I almost snatched it back. But then Soraya nodded, picked up the waterskin, and left. The key grated again in the lock.

Surely there could be no harm in what I'd done. Even if she couldn't be trusted.

For the first time since they had locked me up, I felt a

loosening of the doom that gripped me. A lightening of spirit. Hope.

The day passed slowly. The first of my new candles burned down to a stump; I lighted a second. The moazzen called for prayers at noon and then again at sunset. Each time, I prayed—fervently. Since I couldn't get to water, I had to make dry ablutions, touching the dust on the floor of my room. I was thirsty again, and hungry. My ribs hurt every time I moved, and my whole face ached.

I watched the beetles crawling on the floor, making patterns in the dust. I watched the spiders mending their webs and swaddling unlucky flies. The feeling of doom came back, stronger than before. Would the Khatun keep me in here forever? Would she starve me? Torture me? Would I die here, in this room?

My life—what was left of it—seemed to shrink and harden, like the dry, brittle husk of a rosebud starved for water.

The next morning, sometime after the call for daybreak prayers, I was awakened again by the sound of a key in the lock. As I watched, the door slowly creaked open.

It took a moment for me to make out her features in the glow of my shrinking candle.

Shahrazad.

"Lady!" I exclaimed, then kissed the floor before her. Pain tore at me, but I didn't care.

"Shh, Marjan! Sit up now—don't kiss that dirty floor."

"You shouldn't be here!" I whispered. "The Khatun, she—"

"Don't worry. I have a little time. She sleeps late and—oh, Marjan, look at you!" She knelt down beside me—not worrying about getting her skirts dirty—and fingered the skin around my eye. "Does it hurt?"

I shrugged. "A little."

She opened the bundle she was carrying. Three oranges rolled out; a heap of flatbread and dates and almonds nestled in the cloth. My mouth began to water; hunger reared up within me and raged.

"Eat," Shahrazad said. "This is not the time for politeness. You're probably starved."

Greedily, I reached for a piece of bread. I had to use all the restraint I possessed to keep myself from stuffing the whole thing into my mouth at once. Then I peeled an orange and, putting one section at a time in my mouth, blissfully sucked out the sweet juice.

Shahrazad had brought candles, too, I saw. Five more. And a little pot of salve. This she promptly opened and began to spread the cooling paste beneath my eye. "Now your ribs. Let me see them. Soraya told Dunyazad that you'd been kicked."

"No, Lady, you shouldn't be doing this. I'm your servant, I can—"

"You want me to command you? Is that it? Very well, I command you: Let me see your ribs."

I lifted my gown. In the faint, flickering light I could see that they were bruised—all purple and black. Shahrazad drew in a soft gasp. "Oh, Marjan, I'm so sorry. This is all my fault for bringing you here."

"No, Lady—don't say that! It's not your fault at all. You're saving everyone; you—"

"Shh, Marjan. Just let me do this." Shahrazad began

slathering on the salve. "Have they fed you at all?" she asked.

"Soraya sneaked some food to me yesterday. *That* surprised me."

Shahrazad laughed bitterly. "She approached my sister, told her what had become of you, and lent her the key. It seems Soraya doesn't want my job after all."

"She's afraid," I said. "The Khatun . . . she thinks you've taken a lover. She said she'd think that about any of the Sultan's wives. And so Soraya understood that any wife of the Sultan is . . ."

"Expendable?" Shahrazad said.

I nodded.

"She just realized this?"

"I think . . . she thought she could do what you're doing. I think she envied you."

Shahrazad unrolled a long, clean strip of cloth and began wrapping it around my ribs. "Well, things are going better for me, Marjan—thanks to you. The Sultan loves the story. And we're working on something . . . some way to get you out. My sister has another of her plans." She laughed—not bitterly this time. "It's a good one though," she said. "I don't want to tell you too much because it's—"

"Dangerous to know?" I asked.

"Yes." Shahrazad made a snug knot in the cloth; I smoothed my skirts down around me. "We think we know who your storyteller is," she said, "but I can't tell you that, either. For now . . . there are some gaps in the storyteller's tale. My sister forgot a few parts and I thought maybe you would remember."

"I'll try," I said.

She asked me about Queen Lab's magic rituals and how

long Badar Basim stayed with her and how Queen Lab's mother summoned the jinn. I told her what I remembered.

"Your memory is good," she said.

"No it isn't! I could never remember all the stories you know! Even though I worked for years training my memory—trying to be like you. That's why I started telling stories. Because—" I stopped, feeling suddenly shy. Shahrazad looked at me questioningly; I had to go on. "I admire you so much," I whispered.

Shahrazad bit her lip. I could see that her eyes were glistening. "Marjan," she said. She took one of my hands, enfolded it in hers. "This may be the last time I will ever see you. That's the other reason I had to come—to say good-bye. Someone will come to fetch you—someone you will know you can trust. They'll give you back your comb." She sighed, squeezed my hand. "I'll miss you, my friend. I can never thank you enough for what you've done. I wish I could repay you as it's done in the old tales—with a caravan of mules laden with sacks of gold and silver." She smiled. "But I'll arrange something . . . You won't lack for money. And I'll do everything in my power to get you out of here . . . to a safe place."

My heart was so full, it seemed to swell up into my throat so I could hardly speak. To say good-bye to Shahrazad . . . and to everything I knew. *A safe place.* It would have to be a *strange* place, one that I'd never been to.

"But what about you?" I asked. "What if the Khatun turns the Sultan against you?"

"I don't think she will, Marjan. As long as I keep on with the stories."

"But what if you run out of stories again?"

"I won't. Father will be returning very soon. He's traveling in a caravan with Shahryar's brother, who is coming here to visit. We got word from a courier that they're just a few days away. Before he left, Father promised to bring me many more books with tales from different lands."

But, *How will you* live? I wanted to ask her. *How can you live with a husband you despise, a husband who is a murderer, and will murder* you *for the slightest slip?*

"If only the Sultan would just say you could *live!*" I said. "You've borne him three sons. That should be enough!"

"Shh!" Shahrazad said. "He's wounded, Marjan. He's not ready."

I stared at her. *He* was wounded! What about all the women he'd killed? What about all the lives he'd wrecked? *He* was wounded!

"He *is* wounded, Marjan. His nightmares wake him up; he cries out in his sleep like a frightened child. Part of the reason he likes my stories is they take his mind off his own woes."

"His *sins*, you mean," I said, then was shocked that I had dared say it. But it was *true*.

Shahrazad looked at me for a long moment. Then, "That, too," she said. "He *is* steeped in sin. And he knows it. But he did it out of hurt. He loved his wife, and she betrayed him, and he never wanted to hurt that much again. He's like a wounded little boy who lashes out, and there's no one to teach him how to behave. And he can't overcome his pride to admit that what he did was wrong, and I'm afraid that if I force the issue now, he'll— Well, I dare not. One day, I hope. But not yet."

Something was dawning on me, something so strange

and terrible that I had never even dreamed of it before. "You love him," I said, and I could hear the accusation in my voice.

Shahrazad looked away; the shadows cast a veil over her eyes. When she turned back, her gaze was level. "I'm not ashamed of loving him," she said. "There's nothing wrong with loving someone. It's hating—*that's* what's wrong."

Chapter 19

The Secret Token

Later, after Shahrazad had left, I thought about what she had told me.

The Sultan had nightmares, she had said. He called out in his sleep like a frightened child. I tried to picture that—the Sultan crying out in his sleep like a child.

But I couldn't feel sorry for him. What was there for him to fear, save for himself and his own dark deeds?

Some things that people did were unforgivable. When they murdered innocent women and threatened to kill you if you weren't entertaining enough. When they imprisoned you by magic in a shape not your own and tried to starve you. When they maimed you so that people would pity you for the rest of your life and no one would marry you.

You couldn't forgive those things. *Shouldn't.*

I thought about Shahrazad lying with the Sultan every night. With a *monster.* I had always admired her bravery, outwitting him in his own den. Saving her own life that way—and the lives of countless others. I had never thought . . . that she might *love* him.

How could she love him? How could she *ever* love him?

The room felt empty, now that she was gone. Even emptier than it had been before. My *life* felt empty. I would never see her again.

I peeled my last orange and tried to block out everything except the pleasure of eating it. But my fears and sorrows and resentments kept tumbling around in my mind. My own future was as unseeable as whatever lay beyond the walls of this room. I longed to go back to Uncle Eli and Auntie Chava. But that was impossible. The Khatun could find me there and hurt me. Hurt *them.*

If only I could believe that I had truly saved Shahrazad—or at least that she was better off now than before I had come. But I had put her in greater danger than ever by arousing the Khatun's suspicions. And, though I had given her a few nights of stories, she would still have to find more. In time, she would go through all the new ones her father was bringing. Then what?

Maybe, I thought, the Khatun would kill me after all. Then what would my short life have amounted to? I knelt down and prayed to Allah to save Shahrazad, to save me, to teach me how to live.

Abruptly, I awoke. A sound at the door. A rattling. I scrabbled about to collect the orange peels and candles and stuff them into my sash—ignoring the pangs in my ribs. Then I scooted back to crouch in the far corner of the room.

More rattling. It was the Khatun—I knew it. Or one of her *creatures*. Shahrazad had not said *when* her mysterious friend would come to rescue me, and now the Khatun had made her move first!

Still more rattling. It didn't sound like a key. It didn't scrape as the key had, when Soraya and Shahrazad had come.

Now the door swung silently open. At first, I could see no one in the doorway, no one at all. Is this how the assassins came? Silently? Invisibly? So you never knew until too late?

Then a voice—a small, timid voice.

"Marjan?"

I saw her then, in the weak light of the candle.

"Mitra?" I asked.

She rushed into the room. "Oh, Marjan, I was so scared. Dunyazad taught me how to pick a lock with a midak—they wouldn't give me a key because it would get someone else in trouble. But then it *wouldn't* open, and when it did, I couldn't tell if it was *you* or someone else, it's so dark in here, and— Your eye! Marjan, your eye!"

I had forgotten about my eye, but now that I remembered, it *ached*.

"Shh!" I said. "Mitra, are you the one they sent to get me out?"

"Oh, here. I forgot." She fumbled with something and then held out my comb. "It's the secret token. So you know you can trust me."

Stifling a smile, I took the comb and slipped it into my hair.

"And here. This, too," she said. She handed me a long veil.

I threw it on and, stopping to peer both ways, followed her into the hallway and shut the door softly behind.

It was dark, so dark I could barely see Mitra. I groped with my feet down the stairs, clutched the cool metal railing with one hand. *Quietly!* I told myself. *Don't let your foot clunk.* But now, a pale mist of silver moonlight sifted down around us, growing brighter as we moved into a courtyard.

We skirted the shadowy edge of it and ducked into another dark hallway. So far, no sign of life. I had gone but a few steps into the hall when my foot thunked into a heavy planter and I let out a sharp moan of pain.

A voice: "Who's there?"

"Hurry!" Mitra whispered. We rounded a corner into another hallway; Mitra ducked behind a curtain. I followed—just in time.

The pad of bare feet in the hallway. "Who's there? Show yourself!" A eunuch's voice; I couldn't tell whose. I stood huddling with Mitra, barely breathing, as the footsteps came closer, then moved slowly away.

"The kitchen stairway's over there," Mitra whispered. I couldn't see her, but she took my wrist and pointed it in the direction she meant. "Dunyazad said I'm supposed to tell you, 'Go to Zaynab.' And I'm supposed to say that she will always be grateful."

I hugged Mitra. "I will always be grateful to *you*," I said.

Now I heard more eunuchs' voices from a distance. I opened the curtain a crack, saw no one, then hurried down the dark hallway to the stairs. Just as I reached them, I heard voices coming near. I tiptoed up past the first bend, then stopped so as to make no noise.

"Maybe it was just someone who couldn't sleep," one of the voices was saying.

"I think there were two. I called for them to show themselves, but they wouldn't."

A sigh. "We'd better find them. I'll look—you check on the crippled girl. If *she* escapes, heads will roll."

I waited until I couldn't hear them anymore, then crept up the curved staircase and started across the roof toward the welcoming glow in Zaynab's pavilion. Above, a thousand bright stars pricked the sky; the moon had sunk low in the west. Dawn was not far off. Now Zaynab appeared in the doorway, haloed in light. She made for the edge of the terrace, gesturing for me to *come*.

I moved quickly across the roof to a gap in the railing near the winch, where Zaynab now waited. A few pigeons, slumbering on the railing, fluttered and looked at us curiously. On the floor beside the winch sat a huge raffia basket with two handles. "Get in, my dear!" Zaynab whispered. "I'll lower you to the street. Then go straight to the storyteller's house."

"Do you know him?" I asked.

She hesitated. "I think I knew him once—a long time ago. Now, into the basket. Hurry!"

It was shallow, flimsy looking. The ground seemed far below. I stepped into the basket and sat down inside. I wouldn't think about how frail it was, or how high off the ground. I wouldn't think about the winch, that it was made to carry baskets full of pigeons—not people. I wouldn't think about the streets—how perilous they were at night for a girl all alone. Those things didn't matter. Nothing mattered—except getting *away*.

Zaynab handed me a rolled-up piece of paper and a small, heavy sack. "The coins are for you," she said. "From Shahrazad. The message is from me . . . to your storyteller."

"You . . . wrote it?" I asked.

Zaynab nodded.

Somehow, I had never imagined that she could write! I tucked paper and coins into my sash. Zaynab drew the basket handles together and slipped them through the hook at the end of the rope. "Allah keep all hateful things from you!" she said. Then she scooted the basket—with me in it—over the side of the roof.

Falling. My stomach lurched up into my throat. The winch screeched; a shoal of startled pigeons, cooing and flapping, took flight. Then the rope caught with a jerk and dangled me an arm's length below the edge of the roof.

I could see Zaynab's head and shoulders pumping as she turned the crank. The winch creaked ominously; the basket began to go down. I gazed up into Zaynab's face—memorizing it—until she disappeared behind the lip of the roof.

The rope twisted and squeaked, turning me to face the dark palace walls, then the city, then the walls again. I wrapped my veil close around me. The first blush of daylight softened the eastern horizon, limning the faint outlines of domes and minarets. Away in the distance, the dark green hills hunched against the sky. A feather floated past; I watched it rock down into the shadowed street that rose up to meet me.

A shout from above. A scream. The basket plunged

toward the ground—my stomach leaped up again—then the basket jerked to a swaying halt. When I looked up, I saw a eunuch peering down over the edge of the roof.

More shouting. The basket began to rise. I looked down at the street. I could jump from here—maybe—but I would have to do it *now*. I scooted to one end of the basket, flattening my body so that I could slip beneath the handles, then hung both feet over the edge. The basket tipped and I was sliding, sliding out. At the last moment I panicked and tried to grab hold of the handles, but my hand slipped.

I fell.

My feet hit the ground so hard, they stung. My knees buckled, slammed against stone. I toppled forward, banging an elbow, scraping my hands. Pain gripped my rib cage; for a moment I couldn't breathe. The sack burst open and coins were ringing on the cobblestones, rolling in all directions.

Up on the roof, a eunuch was shouting, pointing down at me.

An answering shout on the street. Someone was coming.

I tried to sweep the coins back into the sack, but my hands were clumsy and stiff. I looked back and saw two helmeted men sprinting toward me. Palace guards. I clutched my veil and ran, too numbed by fear to mourn for my lost fortune or count my injuries. Voices, coming near. I cut into a narrow alley and pressed myself into an alcove by a gate. My heart hammered in my chest; my breath came in ragged gasps. In the street beyond the alley, I saw them running past. I listened until the footfalls grew faint, then fled down the alley.

Now I awoke again to the pain. My left elbow throbbed, my hands and knees burned, my good foot tingled from the impact, and my bad foot had shooting pains.

No matter. *Run.*

If I had been near Auntie Chava and Uncle Eli's house, I would have known which alleys went through to other streets and which ones ended in walls. I would have known shortcuts and back ways to get from here to there. But this part of the city was strange to me. I knew from where the sky grew light that I had come down the eastern face of the palace. And I remembered that the bazaar lay to the south.

So if I went far enough south—to the left—I would come to it. From there, I could find the storyteller's house.

Voices. I ducked into another alley, pressed myself into a niche in the wall until the voices had passed. Then I was off again.

From time to time, I heard them, the voices. When they sounded near, I swerved into doorways or niches or alleys. Once, I tripped over a beggar sleeping in the street; he twitched and moaned. Another time, I saw three men lurking on a street corner. I stopped, backed away silently, cut into the nearest alley, and *ran*. I didn't know which to fear most—the palace guards or the thieves and cutthroats who prowled the streets at night.

Suddenly, I realized that I had stumbled upon the bazaar. It looked different now—dark and naked, stripped of its crowds and colorful wares. The bright canopies, which in daytime gave it a festive air, were rolled up and tied flush to the walls. Stale ghosts of bazaar smells hung in the air. I made my way back to the fountain in the carpet bazaar, and then began to blunder toward the storyteller's house. Quickly, I told myself. Soon would come the call to dawn prayer, and the streets would fill with men hurrying to the mosques. A girl alone would raise questions.

Three times I took a wrong turning, but always I found my way back. I hadn't seen or heard a soul for some time now. At last, I found the corner where Ayaz had always blindfolded me. I hastened through the alley. There was the storyteller's door. Safe!

I knocked.

Nothing. No sound.

I knocked again.

The door opened—just a crack. I saw movement behind it, and then all at once the door swung wide and a man was standing on the step. A jagged, puckered scar ran from his forehead across an eye to his chin. He stared at me with his one good eye, clutching the hilt of a huge scimitar.

Chapter 20
Abu Muslem

LESSONS FOR LIFE AND STORYTELLING

There's more than one way to be crippled. I don't mean that you can have a crippled foot or a crippled knee or a crippled hand. I mean you can be crippled in your heart. You can store up all your rage at someone, which can weigh down on your heart and twist it into a weird shape until you're always aching underneath. After a while you get used to the ache—just like with my foot. You forget what it's like *not* to ache. You forget that you're aching at all.

I turned to flee, but the man gripped me about my waist, lifted me, hoisted me over his shoulder. I squirmed and kicked; it was no use. The door slammed shut. He set me down with a gentleness that surprised me.

"We have a guest," he announced.

Lamplight flared, and in a far, dark corner of the room I saw the storyteller, with Ayaz beside him.

"Little Pigeon?"

The man shifted aside, and the storyteller came toward me with the lamp. "Little Pigeon," he said, "what have they done to you?"

I glanced fearfully at the scar-faced man. He was squat, solidly built, and looked to be of middle years. One eye, the eye the scar cut across, seemed permanently shut.

"It's all right," the storyteller said. "You can trust Kansbar; he's a friend. Now tell me." He lifted the lamp to my face. "Your eye. You're bruised. What's happened?"

All at once, relief flooded through me in a rush so strong that it weakened my knees and took my breath for speech. I had *escaped!* A lump grew in my throat and I thought, for a moment, that I was going to cry. But I didn't. I never cried. When the words finally came, they gushed out: about the Khatun, how she had locked me up. How she wanted to prove that Shahrazad had taken a lover. How she had hit me and kicked me. I told all the way through my escape in the basket and my flight through the streets, and then I went back to Zaynab. "I'm afraid for her," I said. "She'll be punished for helping me escape. The eunuchs—they were with her. Trying to stop her." I remembered the paper she had given me and drew it out of my sash. "You have to help her," I said. "She told me she knew you once, a long time ago."

The storyteller read while Ayaz held the lamp. Kansbar stood sentinel by the door. Shadows flickered across the old man's face; he looked grave. Once he glanced at me, raised his shaggy, pointed brows; then he returned to the letter again. I heard a moazzen call for dawn prayers, but the storyteller made no move to stop reading. Finally he folded the letter, locked it in a chest by the door.

"We'll go now," he said, "to the mosque to pray. You stay here. You can pray in the courtyard but don't open the door to the street. A woman will come to you—I'll give her a key. She'll take you to a safe place. Stay there until I come to fetch you."

"But Zaynab," I said. "Can you help her?"

"I'll do what I can."

"Wait," Ayaz said. He disappeared through the curtain into the adjoining room and returned with a small copper jar. "Here." He thrust the jar into my hands.

It was heavy for its size; I nearly dropped it. I looked inside and saw coins. It was full of coins. This was his cache that he had greedily hoarded—probably all his life.

"I . . . can't take this," I said.

Ayaz huffed out an impatient sigh. "Well, you wouldn't have to if you hadn't foolishly dropped those ones Zaynab gave you. But now that you have . . . you'll need them."

I glanced at the storyteller. He was smiling oddly, looking at Ayaz. Then he turned to me.

"The coins *will* help you," he said.

Still I hesitated.

"It's a loan!" Ayaz said. "You didn't think I was giving them to you, did you? You'd better be prepared to pay me back. Next time . . . next time we meet."

And then he was out the door, the storyteller and the scar-faced man behind him. I heard the grating of the key in the lock, and then their retreating footsteps. "Thank you," I whispered.

I went out into the small, shadowed yard, made ablutions in a pond, and prayed. Then I sat down inside to wait. The lamp, which Ayaz had set on the chest by the door, cast a pool of light on the chest lid. And in that light . . . lay the key.

It would be wrong to look inside. The storyteller was helping me, and that would be breaching his trust.

But then . . . How did I *know* he was helping me? I knew nothing about him! What if he was not like the good-magician grocer in the tale, but one of the Khatun's creatures instead?

Still, I had an idea about who he might be. If I knew for certain I was right, it would set my mind at ease.

What harm would it do to look?

I took the lamp off the chest and set it on the floor. Kneeling, I inserted the key, felt it lift the pins in the lock. I raised the lid.

There, lying atop some dark, old robes, was Zaynab's letter. I took it out, unrolled it, held it to the lamp.

I'm not very good at reading. My mother tried to teach me years ago, but we didn't get far enough for me to read anything interesting, like a story. There were some words on this letter that I remembered. I saw my own name, *Marjan*, five times. And another word leaped out at me, because it was the word I was looking for.

Vizier.

I tried to find some words I knew near *vizier*, but I couldn't. Zaynab's handwriting was cramped and hard to read, and the ink had smeared in a few places, and the words reminded me of city streets—only much straighter—with rows of little buildings, and funny, upside-down domes, and tiny, waving banners, and even birds flying overhead. But *vizier*. I could read that.

The Sultan's old vizier, the one his father had before him, had known him since he was a boy. The vizier might have told him some stories. Maybe he had made up some of them, which is why no one had ever heard the Julnar story before. And then the old vizier was banished, Shahrazad had said, because he had gone against the Sultan in the matter of killing wives. And now here was this storyteller, telling a tale that no one but he and the Sultan seemed to have heard. And he knew of Zaynab. And Zaynab had sent him a message. A long message.

I wished I could remember that old vizier's name. Maybe I could find it in the note. It would be somewhere near the beginning. But I couldn't read that part.

I was about to put the letter back inside the chest, when I noticed a glinting in a corner. I pulled aside the dark robes and there it was, a length of purple fabric, embroidered with gold thread. I drew it out, unfolded the cloth.

It was a robe of honor, such as the Sultan gives to his most esteemed retainers.

A rattling at the door.

Quickly, I folded the robe, tucked it beneath the others, then threw in Zaynab's letter and shut the chest lid. Just in time. A creaking of hinges; a veiled woman slipped through the doorway.

"Hurry!" she said. "Come with me."

I reached for the copper jar Ayaz had given me, but the woman was shaking her head. "No. Leave the jar. You can take coins, but no other possessions. Abu Muslem forbids it."

Abu Muslem?

"Hurry!"

I poured the coins into my sash, trying to separate them so they wouldn't clink together. The woman shooed me out the door, locked it behind us, then led me by a twisting route through the poor neighborhoods of the city. My mind was churning. *Abu Muslem.* What did this have to do with Abu Muslem? Did she think I was one of the women he was smuggling out of the city? But why would she think that? Unless . . .

Unless the storyteller was Abu Muslem.

But what about Badar Basim and Zaynab and the robe of honor? Who but the old vizier could twist those three strands into a single thread?

And then I knew. I felt stupid I had never thought of it before.

The storyteller and the old vizier and Abu Muslem were one and the same.

I watched for landmarks in the slanting morning light along the way—a bird's nest in a chink in the wall, a carved cornice above a doorway, a street where the walls were made of red stone. At last, we stopped at a rough-hewn courtyard door. The woman knocked. The door opened a crack; she spoke to someone, then shooed me inside. "Allah protect you, Sister," she said. The door closed behind me.

"This way. Come." A thin woman with a long braid called over her shoulder. She had already begun to walk—wearily, I thought—across the courtyard. It was a poor courtyard, much poorer than Auntie Chava's had been. A few scrawny chickens clucked and fluttered as I came near. A bony donkey stood tethered to a stake. When I entered the cool darkness inside the cracked mud house, the woman motioned me to sit.

"Are you thirsty? Would you like a drink of water?"

"Yes, if you please," I said.

The woman moved deep into the shadows. I could see her pouring, could hear water gurgling into a cup. She handed it to me; I took off my veil. When I had finished, I saw that she was staring at me. "It is good to see you, Marjan," she said. "Do you remember me at all?"

At first I thought, with a wild hope that surprised me—that startled me, in fact—that she might be my mother. That there had been some mistake and she hadn't died after all.

But she was not my mother. I could see that now. She was about the age that I remembered my mother, but her gaunt face, with its small mouth and eyes that turned down at the corners, was not my mother's face.

I shook my head then, *no*. Though there *was* something familiar about her. Something I couldn't place.

"Who are you?" I asked.

"I am Farah. I was your mother's serving girl before she died."

My heart seemed to freeze in my chest. *Farah.* So long it had been since I had met anyone who knew my mother. And my mother had been fond of Farah. Had she been my mother's only friend? I could see them now in memory, smiling together over something I had said or done. Farah had a low voice that I had found comforting, and kindly, serious eyes.

"There are some things," she said now, "that I would like to tell you. About your mother."

"I don't want to hear about her."

A soft cry sounded from a dark corner of the room. I looked and saw two children—one an infant, the other not much older—asleep on a single straw pallet.

"I've known the man they call Abu Muslem for many years," Farah said. "I told him about you when I first learned who he is, a year after your mother died. He came to me this morning to tell me some things he had read about you in a letter. I think you *need*, Marjan, to hear about your mother."

I looked away, pretending not to listen, while she told me how, after my father died, my mother became the fourth wife of Aga Jamsheed and took me to live with her in his harem. I knew that already. But then she told me some things I didn't know. "Aga Jamsheed was drunk with love for your mother," Farah said. "He favored her above his other wives, which made them hate her." When the Sultan began killing wives, Farah said, my mother began to pester Aga Jamsheed to take us out of the city, so that I would be in no danger from the Sultan. "Aga Jamsheed said there was nothing to worry about, that you were too young. But your mother wasn't satisfied. 'Who knows how long he'll keep killing his wives?' your mother said. 'One of these days, he'll run out of young women and start marrying children!' She begged Aga Jamsheed to find Abu Muslem, to have him smuggle you and her out of the city. Aga Jamsheed refused. In time, he grew tired of her nagging. He commanded her to stop. But your mother would not. She loved you more than anything. More than food. More than water."

The old anger spurted up inside me, filling my chest, pushing against the base of my throat. I pulled back my skirts, pointed to my crippled foot. "Is *this* love?" I demanded. "Is *this* what you call love?"

Farah met my gaze. "Surely that's not all you remember," she said. "You wouldn't have heard how she fought for you—she was very careful about that, but . . . Don't you remember the stories? She used to hold you in her lap for half the day, telling you stories she had made up especially for you. And some of your favorites she told over and over again—a thousand and one times!"

And it came back to me now, against my will: how it

felt to snuggle in my mother's lap, warm and protected, while her voice led me on wild, fantastical adventures.

"The quarrels grew louder and more spiteful," Farah went on, "until Aga Jamsheed grew to loathe her. His other wives were pleased and agreed with all the bad things he said about her.

"One night, your mother overheard him talking to his brother. He would divorce her, he said. And to spite your mother, he would sell you as a slave into the Sultan's household.

"I don't know if he truly would have done that. I don't think so. But things were so bad between him and your mother, she was sure he would. That's why she did what she did. It was a terrible thing. But she was desperate. It was all she could think to do."

"She should have run away with me!" I said. "She should have escaped from the harem and gone to Abu Muslem!"

"She couldn't," Farah said. "Aga Jamsheed kept a guard at the gate, and none of the women were allowed out without his permission."

"She should have thought of something else—like Shahrazad! *She* didn't just give up."

"Marjan. Not everybody can be as clever as Shahrazad."

"She shouldn't have killed herself! That was the easy way for *her!* She should have stayed with me. I *needed* her to protect me!"

"Listen. They would have killed her anyway for what she did to your foot. The Sultan had forbidden the practice of maiming girls to keep them from becoming his wives. The penalty was death. So she . . ." Farah pursed her lips, gazed up at the sky. She breathed in deep. "Well," she sighed, looking back at me. "You know what she did. And afterward . . . Aga Jamsheed was afraid *he* would be punished for permitting you to be maimed. So he hired you out to the Jew. Then he and his family left the city.

"That's what I wanted to tell you, Marjan. Blame your mother for provoking her husband, for mistaken judgment of his character. Don't blame her for leaving you to go on without her, or for not fighting hard enough. She was brave, Marjan. She *fought*. And everything she did was for you. She *cherished* you. She cherished you above everything."

I had the strangest feeling, then, as if my heart were softening in my chest. I could feel the blood pumping warm and fast into my arms and face and legs. I was crying then, crying for my mother, crying that I had lost her, crying that I had nursed my rage against her for so long. I was crying for Zaynab, and for Shahrazad, and for the dead girl who had lived in my room. I was crying for *all* the women who had died, all the misery that had come over this whole city because the Sultan's first wife had hurt *him*.

It seemed that in this world we were piling up hurt upon hurt, and hate upon hate, and then hurt upon hurt again. Forgiveness. We couldn't forgive. We could only hate when we were hurt. And then the hurt and the hate would start up again—all in a terrible circle.

Chapter 21
A Desperate Plan

That night, I had a dream about Badar Basim. He was an old man, and he was walking down a garden path with an old woman, and the old woman was Princess Jauharah, now his queen. Badir Basim was limping. He winced when he trod on his left foot, and his brow was furrowed with pain.

They came to a bench and sat down together. Badir Basim took off his left boot and I saw that his foot—this one foot—had never turned all the way back from when Princess Jauharah had changed him into a bird. It was a bird's foot—all orange and skinny and knobbly.

And then, as I watched in my dream, Princess Jauharah knelt down on the ground before Badir Basim and began to massage his foot. She kneaded it—caressed it—and the pain eased from his face.

❖   ❖   ❖

When I awoke the next morning, I sat up fast, startled because I didn't recognize where I was. It was a small, dark room, like my room at Auntie Chava's. A jumble of household goods surrounded the straw mattress I slept on: chipped clay pots, a pair of woven saddlebags, a coil of rope, a rickety loom. This was a storage room. Then I remembered. Escaping from the harem. Zaynab. The storyteller-vizier-Abu Muslim. Farah.

My mother.

Who had loved me. Cherished me, Farah had said. And she had fought for me, too. Hard.

It was *she* who had taught me to love stories, stories she had made up herself. How had I forgotten that? How had I forgotten those journeys I'd taken, riding on the waves of her voice?

It would have been better, as things turned out, if she had obeyed Aga Jamsheed. But she couldn't have known that Shahrazad was going to save all the girls in the city—which she still might not be able to do. Also, my mother probably wasn't as clever as Shahrazad, nor as wise. But who was? Why should I have expected that of her?

She was my *madar*, and she was brave, and she had protected me the only way she knew how.

Farah lived with her husband, who gathered thornbrush in the forest outside the city and sold it as firewood in the bazaar. Her two squalling babies, once awake, would calm to neither stories nor singing nor rocking. Her husband had left by the time I arose, and Farah was hard at work lugging pails of water from the neighborhood well. When I offered to help with the hauling, she said no, that

I mustn't go outside the gate. She poured me a cup of water and handed me a small loaf of barley bread. Then she scooped up a potful of lentils and asked me to pick out the bugs and grit.

I helped her all that day—tending the babies, spinning, sieving grain, scrubbing floors, patching the little ones' tattered gowns. Farah seemed sad that I had grown so adept at doing menial chores, as she called them. "Your mother's heart would break," she said. Still, I could tell that she was grateful for the help.

They were poor—much poorer than Auntie Chava. Farah's face looked lined and bleak; she had no relations to help her. The babies, I soon discovered, squalled because they were hungry. When Farah nursed them, they would suck greedily for a short time, and then turn away from her breasts and cry. Not enough milk. And the family couldn't afford a goat. The chickens were gaunt, the stores of lentils and grains woefully low.

Farah's husband returned late that night. She shooed me into the tiny storeroom as he entered the courtyard. Afterward, I heard them arguing. "She's dangerous!" the husband shouted. "If we're caught with her, they'll kill us." Farah's voice rose in gentle protest, but I couldn't make out her words. I crept to the door and opened it a crack to hear better.

". . . the pigeon keeper at the palace," Farah's husband was saying. "They found messages from Abu Muslem in her pavilion. They know who he is now. He's the Sultan's old vizier, the one he banished. I heard they tortured the pigeon keeper to get her to say where he is and who else is in on the plot."

"Did she tell?" Farah asked.

"How would I know? If they find the girl here, they'll torture *us!* She can't stay!"

"But I owe this to her mother. Just two more days, Abu Muslem said. What will become of her if we throw her into the street?"

"You are too softhearted, my wife. Think of your own safety. Think of your sons. If anything were to happen to you . . ." It was silent then, for a moment, except for a rustling of fabric and a soft sigh. Then the husband's voice came again. "I'll give her tonight. Tomorrow she goes."

Carefully, I shut the door. A cold hand was closing around my heart. I had hoped for too much from the storyteller. I had thought he could somehow put things right. But now . . . Zaynab tortured! Because of messages from Abu Muslem.

Would they kill her if she didn't tell where he was?

Did she even *know* where he was?

I wouldn't stay until Farah's husband put me out on the street. I had to leave tonight.

I waited until the household was still, until I could hear Farah's husband snoring. I pushed aside the blanket and, kneeling on my pallet, untied the bundle I had made of my sash. I groped my way to where the food jars stood and buried the coins in the shallow cache of lentils.

I couldn't do anything for my mother. But I could do *this*—for her friend.

For just a moment, I allowed myself to imagine Farah finding the coins—the surprise and wonder on her face. I imagined all the food jars overflowing, a plump wet nurse feeding the babies, and a servant helping Farah with her work. Whether there would be enough coins to pay for all of that, I didn't know. But it made a good picture in my mind.

I drew on my veil and picked up my sandals but didn't put them on. Then I slipped out the courtyard gate.

The moon hung low over the city as I made my way through the narrow streets, watching for the landmarks I had impressed upon my memory. I stopped to put on my sandals and, a little while later, found myself at the corner where Ayaz had blindfolded me twice. I stumbled eagerly down the dark alley, hope swelling suddenly within me. Maybe the storyteller had a plan to save Zaynab. He *wouldn't* let her die.

I tapped at the door.

No answer.

"It's Marjan," I said softly. "Let me in."

Still no answer.

I pushed at the door. Silently, it swung open.

Quiet. Not a listening quiet or a sleeping quiet. An empty quiet.

In the moonlight that trickled in through the open doorway, I could see that the room was bare. No carpets, no lamp, no chest.

They had gone.

I slumped down on the hard tiled floor, feeling betrayed. They had *had* to leave, I told myself. It was too dangerous for them here now. They had arranged for me. Two days from now, someone would have come to take me to a safe place.

But in two days, it might be too late for Zaynab. They had connected her to Abu Muslem—and me to her. And, since everyone knew that Shahrazad had summoned me to the harem, it would not take long to attach *her* to the string. To connect her to the traitor the Sultan had been trying for years to catch.

Think, I told myself.

The truth, which we had tried so hard to hide, wasn't nearly as bad as what Shahrazad would stand accused of now. And yet the truth, with Shahrazad's little deceptions, would probably enrage the Sultan.

Still, I remembered something Shahrazad had told me, about framing dangerous truths inside of tales within tales. And I formed a desperate plan.

It was all I could think to do.

Chapter 22

The Sultan

It was some time after daybreak when I turned onto a wide avenue and saw the palace's main entrance looming before me. The streets had begun to fill with people, so I was not as conspicuous as before. It had taken me a long time to get there. I had come by a roundabout route— keeping to alleys as much as possible, hiding in niches or ducking around corners when I heard footsteps.

Since I *was* going back, it would be better to do it of my own free will than to be hauled in by the harem guards. Better to go straight to the Sultan than to be delivered into the hands of the Khatun.

A strange calmness filled me as I broke off from the crowd in the streets and approached the palace guards. I half expected them to rush forward and seize me, but they only stood and watched.

"I am Marjan, Shahrazad's slave," I said. "I escaped from the harem and have come back to surrender to the Sultan. And to tell him a story—one he'll want to hear."

They handed me over to two guards inside, who prodded me with their spears and marched me through the tiled courtyard I had crossed with Auntie Chava. We did not go through the harem doors, but veered right instead, through the doors to the royal assembly hall, where the Sultan governed. We passed through rooms of breathtaking beauty, and everywhere we went, men wearing richly colored silk gowns stopped to stare.

At last, we came to a high golden door with two guards before it. The four guards spoke softly among themselves. They didn't want to interrupt the Sultan, but, "They're looking for her," one of them said. Beyond, in the chamber, I could hear voices arguing.

Now one of the guards opened the door and slipped inside. The voices swelled, and then a single voice—deep and rolling—broke in, stilled the others.

"Yes. What is it?"

"We have the girl who escaped, my lord. She surrenders to you . . . and requests to tell you a story."

A rippling murmur inside the chamber.

"Let her come in," the deep voice said.

The guard flung the door wide. The huge room lay before me, with windows of colored glass, cloth-of-gold hangings, carved ceilings taller than full-grown trees. At the far end, a man sat on a throne in the midst of a group of standing people. His black silk robes were edged in sable; he wore an enormous ruby in his turban and a diamond-studded dagger at his waist.

The Sultan.

All at once, my calmness vanished, and I wanted nothing so much as to turn and run from the room.

I walked as gracefully as I could. The whole room blurred before me, except for the Sultan's face. I knelt before him, kissed the carpet at his feet. I was trembling.

"*That* one!" The Khatun's voice. "Shahrazad's cripple, the go-between for your queen"—her voice dripped with disdain—"and this traitor."

"Rise," the Sultan said.

I got slowly to my feet, glancing at the Sultan. His eyes were hard. Quickly, I looked over the group, picking out the Khatun and, beside her, Soraya. There were two men I did not recognize, an older one and a younger one. The younger one resembled the Sultan. His brother, I thought. His brother from the land of Samarkand, who had also been killing a wife every night. Then, in a shadowed far corner, surrounded by guards, I found the one I was looking for. *This traitor.* The storyteller—Abu Muslem. Had he come to help Zaynab? His hands were bound, I saw. But what surprised me was that beside him—also bound and guarded—stood the gold-clad eunuch.

"So. You want to tell me a story," the Sultan said.

"Yes, my lord." It came out as a scared whisper.

"I'm glad *someone* is willing to talk," he said, his voice heavy with sarcasm. "My pigeon keeper won't. Nor will these two"—he jerked his head toward the storyteller and the gold-clad eunuch—"confess to me what trouble they've been stirring up. So now I am curious. Is this a true tale you came to tell?"

"There is truth *in* the tale, my lord."

"Indeed." He narrowed his eyes; I looked down at the floor. "And what does it treat with?" he asked.

"It treats, my lord, with a poor boy, the servant of a powerful magician." My voice was still shaky and soft. I forced myself to speak louder. "Every day he would go to the sea with his master. The magician would cast his fishing net and call out a magical word. Then the fish would puff themselves up into balls and float up through the water, entangling themselves in the net, until the magician called out another magical word. Then—"

"This is an outrage!" The Khatun lurched toward me. "My son, let me deal with this girl. She has the effrontery to burst in here and turn your mind from important affairs of state with a piece of fluff about enchanted *fish*. She's a harem slave—my responsibility. I'll wring a *true* story out of her."

The Sultan held up his hand. "Wait. We'll come to that. This girl escaped my guards and was safely away, but returned because she wanted to tell me this tale. It amuses me. You know I like stories," he said, his mouth twisting into a joyless smile, "and I have not heard this one before."

I knew he hadn't heard it, because I had made it up. I couldn't risk boring him with one he'd already heard. Anyway, my mother made up tales. It was in my blood.

"But," the Sultan warned me, "you won't leave this room without telling what mischief you have been up to, and why you escaped."

"I will, my lord."

"Very well. Go on."

I told how the magician's boy decided to fish for himself, but he forgot the second magic word. When the fish puffed themselves into balls and rose up into the air, the boy snatched at the cords of the net, tried to pull it down. But the fish carried him aloft, and soon he was too high up in the air to let go. They floated through the sky, over the green hills, and into a far-off country. At last the fish wafted down and landed in the shallows of a pond in a beautiful garden.

"Just then," I said, "the owner of the garden spied the boy and summoned his guards. He was going to kill the boy for stealing into his garden. The boy pleaded for his life, and at last, the landlord said, 'If you can tell me a story I have never heard before, I will let you live.'"

The sound of a throat clearing. I looked up and caught the Khatun's eye. She was glaring at me, arms folded before her. I peeked at the Sultan; I couldn't tell what he was thinking. But he didn't stop me, so I went on in a rush.

"Now it happened that the fish had been talking as they floated through the sky, and the boy had understood them. He thought surely the landlord would not have heard of what the fish discussed, and so he told them *that* story, about a merman, a king of the sea—"

"This king was not . . . Badar Basim?" the Sultan interrupted.

"No," I said. "This was another merman. Even more illustrious and powerful than Badar Basim. The ruler of all the creatures in the sea."

The Sultan made a tent of his fingers, tapped the tips of them together. "Go on," he said.

I took a deep breath to calm my trembling voice. This was the scary part. What would the Sultan do when I held up my story's mirror and showed him his own reflection? I told how the merman king was married to a beautiful mermaid, but she betrayed him. "So he had her executed, and he vowed to marry a new mermaid every night and chop off her head the next morning, so that no wife of his would ever betray him again."

The Sultan leaped to his feet. "This tale cuts too close!" he roared. The guards shifted toward me.

My heart stood still, but I stood my ground, trying to seem unafraid. I shrugged. "It's only a tale," I said, "that the fish told. The landlord was amused, and I thought you might be, too."

The Sultan slowly settled himself back against the cushions. "*Go . . . on*," he said grimly.

I continued. "It all happened as he had said, until one night the merman king married a beautiful mermaid who sang to him a wondrous song. It had many verses, though, and there wasn't time for her to complete it before morning dawned and the king had to attend to his prayers and his duties to his subjects. So he gave her stay until the next night—"

"Stop her!" The Khatun shoved forward and stood beside me; the sickly-sweet smell of her filled my nose. "My son! Can't you see what she's doing? She *mocks* you!"

"*Do* you mock me?" the Sultan growled.

"No. No, my lord. I only—"

"Let me take her now! Don't demean yourself to be mocked."

The Sultan snapped his fingers and two guards seized my arms.

"One moment, noble king!" I felt the weight of all the eyes in the room staring at me for my audacity. "I thought you might like to know, my lord, in what way the singing mermaid . . . *deceived* . . . her husband."

"Wait," the Sultan said to the guards. Even the Khatun was silent.

"It was a small thing," I said, "but one that brought her much grief."

The Sultan stared at me for what seemed a very long time. I kept my gaze down at the floor. I was hot, uncomfortably hot. My bloodbeat pounded in my ears. Finally, at the edges of my sight, I saw the Sultan nod at the guards; they loosed my arms but stood close at either side of me. "Go on," the Sultan said. His voice was soft now. Ominous.

I plunged in. "It was soon after she had borne him his third son, my lord. She was weak from childbearing and fuddled from lack of sleep." I told of how the queen mermaid was at a loss for a song that night, and how her sister brought her a poor serving maid from the far reaches of the kingdom. "A mermaid with a broken fin," I said. "She swam a little crooked. But she liked to sing songs." Not very subtle, perhaps, but I didn't have a thousand nights to make my meaning clear. Then I told how the broken-finned mermaid sang the queen a song, and how the queen sang it to the king, and how he liked it and asked for more verses of that same song. And then I told how the queen, eager to please, had promised it to him.

"She said that she knew it, my lord. She was eager to please him. But she didn't know the rest of the song. *That* was her deception."

I kept my eyes downcast and held my breath, awaiting his wrath.

"So this mermaid with the . . . broken fin," he said slowly. "*She* knew the rest of the song?"

I glanced at the Sultan, then, but I couldn't read his face. It was closed. A mask of stone.

"No," I said. "But she had heard the first part years before from a . . . a singer in the bazaar. And she thought that he would know it, and that she might find him."

I told, then, how the queen had smuggled the girl out twice (I left Dunyazad out of it) to find the rest of the song. I ended it happily, talking fast so that no one would break in before I got to the end. "So the merman king forgave his queen. And he honored her above all other women. He told her that henceforth she needed only sing for the joy of it. He would never compel her again. And he would never, ever slay her. And then," I said, "the compassionate landlord showed mercy on the magician's apprentice. 'You have indeed entertained me with a tale I have never heard before,' he said. He gave him a mule and some fruit from his garden, and he sent him on his way home."

When I had finished, I stood looking down at the carpet. It was done now. I had either saved Shahrazad or condemned her.

"She *lies*," the Khatun said.

"Hmm." The Sultan's voice. At the edge of my vision I could see that he was tapping his fingers again. "And this . . . mermaid queen didn't know that the storyteller was Abu Muslem?"

"No! She didn't have the least suspicion, my lord."

"Hmm." He spoke softly, as if to himself. "So. If your

tale has truth in it, my old vizier would not only be Abu Muslem—he would be your singer-in-the-bazaar as well. Which would make sense—now that I think on it—for it was he who told me Julnar's tale when I was a boy. He must have written to Zaynab, whom he had known in the past, for reasons of . . . romance or conspiracy, I know not which. Then, when he heard she'd been arrested, he tried to rescue her, aided by my chief harem eunuch. And they were caught." The Sultan turned to the storyteller. "Well?" he demanded. "Do I have it right?"

The storyteller met his gaze. Then, "Yes, my lord," he said.

"So. Now that this girl has taught you what to say, you're willing to talk. Is that it?"

The storyteller said nothing.

The Sultan sighed. "Well, it does fit together. But I don't know if it's true." He turned to the younger man standing beside him. "You see my dilemma, brother," he said. "What would you do in my position?"

"Ask for proof," the brother said. "For witnesses."

"Hmm," the Sultan said again. He regarded me thoughtfully. "Can anyone verify your story? Except for these"—he looked at the storyteller and the gold-clad eunuch—"whom I no longer trust."

I hesitated. I would *not* bring Dunyazad into it. Her word would be suspect, anyway. The same with Zaynab.

"She's lying and I can prove it," the Khatun said. "I don't know about Abu Muslem—though I'm certain Shahrazad was plotting treason with him. But it was a *man* they smuggled in and out of the harem—not this girl. It was your precious wife's lover. I saw them together, and I'm not the only one."

"There was no lover! My daughter would never do that!" It was the old man I had noticed before. He must be the vizier, Shahrazad's father.

"There *was!*" the Khatun insisted. "I saw him with my own eyes and so did Soraya. Tell him, Soraya."

Soraya blanched. I could almost see her weighing sides, calculating which one held the least danger. Then, "I never saw . . . a man, my lord," she said.

"What!" The Khatun, livid, glowered at Soraya. "She's a liar. She's lying to save her neck, just like the cripple!"

"It seems to me," the Sultan said slowly, "that they're putting their necks on the block. This one"—he looked at me—"came out of a safe hiding place to tell me why she sneaked out of my harem. That one"—he turned to Soraya—"risks *your* wrath, which is nearly as renowned as mine."

The Sultan tapped his tented fingers, staring into the distance. Suddenly, he lunged toward me, took hold of my wrist, and pulled me roughly down to sit on the cushion beside him. "This . . . mermaid," he said through clenched teeth, leaning in so close to me that I could smell the mint on his breath. "The one who sang to the king at night." His voice was fierce, but quiet. I couldn't tell if anyone but me could hear. "How . . ." he began. "How did she think of the king . . . in her heart?"

I glanced quickly up at his face and saw there a look that took me by surprise. An oddly soft, vulnerable, hurting look. The look of a man who might cry out in his sleep at night, like a child. But then the stony mask slid back.

"Did she despise him," the Sultan asked, "for making her sing for her life each night? Did she only *pre-*

tend affection to save her own skin? Did she . . . loathe him for what he had done before, to his other wives? For his . . . sins?"

"No, my lord," I said softly. "She loved him."

"Do you *swear* it?" He gripped my wrist harder, until it hurt.

"Yes, my lord. She told me—" I stopped, corrected myself. "She told the mermaid with the broken fin. She said the king—the *merman* king, my lord—she said that he had a deep hurting inside him. She said that she wanted to soothe him. And when the mermaid with the broken fin . . . *questioned* how the queen could love him—because of the things you just said, my lord—the queen said, 'I'm not ashamed of loving him. There's nothing wrong with loving someone. It's hating—that's what's wrong.'"

I glanced at him again. Pain was flooding his eyes. A spasm shuddered across his countenance, and the stone facade broke. Crumbled. The muscles in his face were working, struggling for control. He bowed his head, covered his face with his hands, and I heard a sharp intake of breath that might have been a sob.

It was quiet in the room. No one looked at the Sultan, and we all avoided one another's eyes.

All but the Khatun. She was staring at her son, alarmed.

At last, he pulled his hands away from his face. He had composed it again into the mask.

"You still have no certain proof, either way," his brother reminded him.

The Sultan nodded.

"Proof?" The Khatun said. "You don't believe your

own mother? Who gave birth to you? Who nursed you? Who protected you from assassins all your life? Who—"

"Gracious mother," the Sultan said. "You have done all of those things. For that, I will honor you forever. But now . . ." He looked about the room. "I need to hear one more story. From Shahrazad. Just the two of us, alone. So leave me now—all of you."

"But what will you do about *them*?" the Khatun demanded, pointing at me, then the storyteller, then the eunuch.

The Sultan looked at us as if he had forgotten us completely. "Oh," he said. "Well, they've all conspired to deceive me. Guards, take them to the dungeon. Lock them up."

Chapter 23
The Green Hills

LESSONS FOR LIFE AND STORYTELLING

Every storyteller has a special way she likes to end her tales. My mother used to say, *And now my story has come to an end, but the sparrow never got home*—even if there wasn't any sparrow in her story. Other tellers like to end with a rhyme. For instance:

Mulberry, Mulberry
Here ends my story.

The storytellers in the bazaar are known for dropping hints about something they'd like you to give them:

And now my story I have told
And though I would not ask for gold . . .
Silver dihrams, copper fils
Would happily reward my skills.

When you hear those words—those ending words—you know that's all there is.

But real life isn't like that. Its endings are squirmier than the ones in stories. You try to tuck them in neatly and they kick the blankets off.

The thing about life is, no matter what happens to you, it goes on. What seems like an ending is really a beginning in disguise.

The guards herded us down a long, narrow flight of stairs to a hallway lined with wooden doors. About halfway down the hall, they unlocked one and shoved me into a dark cell. I heard the key grate in the lock, then footfalls, then the clunk of another door.

At first I thought I was alone.

In the shaft of dusty sunlight that streamed in through a high, small window, I could see iron rings mounted on the stone walls. The floors were also of stone—rough and uneven, full of sand and dirt. It stank.

In a corner of the cell, the shadows clotted into a solid form: a woman rising slowly to her feet.

"Marjan? I thought you got away. Oh, my dear!"

Zaynab!

I ran to her; she held me in her arms. She smelled of feathers, a dusty, comfortable smell. "Did they hurt you?" I asked.

"Oh, it did hurt. But it's stopped hurting now."

"Well, you can tell them anything they want to know. Just *tell* them, so they won't hurt you. I told the Sultan everything this morning. Except about Dunyazad. We can't tell about her." I related what had happened since I had left the palace—how I found the storyteller and discovered that he was both the old vizier and Abu Muslem. How Farah had told me about my mother. How I'd left her and couldn't find the storyteller, so I'd come back and told my story to the Sultan.

"Did he believe you?" Zaynab asked. "Is he going to pardon Shahrazad?"

"I don't know. I thought so, for a moment. He said he's going to talk to her alone. But then he sent me and the storyteller and the chief harem eunuch down here. Because we deceived him."

"He said that? *Deceived?*"

I nodded.

Zaynab closed her eyes, shaking her head.

"I hope I haven't . . . Oh, if I've sent her to her death—"

"Don't think that, my dear! You haven't! Of course you haven't."

"When do you think we'll know?" I said. "About what will happen . . . after he talks to Shahrazad?"

Zaynab sighed. "I don't know. Maybe not till morning. That's when they used to announce a new wife. We'll hear the bells."

"And if we hear nothing—"

"That will be good news."

The day crawled past. We waited. Listened. A eunuch came, bringing food and sharbat, but he refused to answer our questions. Still, "Sharbat!" Zaynab said wonderingly. "This is the first I've had sharbat in this cell."

I asked her some things I had been wondering about the storyteller. She told me that they had worked together when she was the governor of the messenger pigeons and he was vizier. They had not been friends, exactly, but there had been respect between them. After he had been banished, the vizier and Zaynab had corresponded several times by carrier pigeon until the Sultan replaced Zaynab for a short time with a man. "It ended there," she said. "I never heard from him again. I never knew that he was Abu Muslem, until he told me in his messages after you delivered him the birds."

"But he must have liked you," I said, remembering

what the Sultan had said about romance. "Or he wouldn't have risked his life trying to rescue you."

"Rescue?" She blinked at me, puzzled.

"You didn't know? He was in the room when I told the story. Bound and gagged, with the gold-clad eunuch." Who must have been the inside helper, I thought. *Not* the soft-faced one. "They're down here, too, locked up."

Zaynab looked sad and thoughtful. "Maybe he thought that if you and I were gone, there would be no one to tell what Shahrazad had done. Maybe he trusted that she would be clever enough to get herself out of trouble, as long as there were no witnesses."

Or maybe he liked you, I thought.

Late in the afternoon came the sounds we had been dreading. Bells.

I sat stricken, numb with dread.

"Wait," Zaynab said. "Listen."

In the distance, I heard the faint call of a crier. There was news.

"They don't usually have a crier for a new wife," Zaynab said. "It might be something else."

The crier's voice drew nearer, until—finally!—I could understand:

"His Royal Magnificence, Shahryar, wishes to invite all of his subjects to the celebration of his marriage to his beloved queen, Shahrazad."

Later, Zaynab and I wished that we had listened to the rest of the message. It had gone on, but we were so full of joy and dancing that we hadn't heard a word.

Celebration of his marriage. They had never celebrated their marriage. Back then, nearly three years ago, the Sultan had been marrying a new wife every night and there hadn't been time for celebration. But now . . . a belated celebration. That was good. It sounded . . . permanent.

I pictured in my mind what would happen when Shahrazad came to get us. We would kneel before her, but she would raise us up, embracing us, thanking us profusely. She would lead us in a jubilant procession to the Sultan, who would thank us gravely and present us with gold and jewels and robes of honor. Then we would be borne up on a litter and paraded through the streets, where people would smile and wave and pelt us with rose petals.

But Zaynab took a more sober view. She tried to comfort me, patting my hand and calling me *my dear* and telling me everything would be all right. But I could see that she was worried. Finally, I got her to tell me what she was thinking. "I'm afraid," she said, "that the Sultan may not know what to do with us. You left the harem, and I helped. And we both had dealings with Abu Muslem. Shahrazad will try to help us—help *you*, anyway. But the Sultan is . . . stern. He may feel he has to make an example of us and your storyteller. To show that people can't get away with defying him."

Over the following days and nights, many sounds drifted down to us in our cell: strains of flutes and drums and cymbals, joyful singing, bell ringings, and, more and more as time went by, the dull roar of many voices.

Zaynab told me that in all her days at the palace she had never heard of a celebration as grand as this one seemed to be. "There are *so* many voices," she said. "And the music never stops."

I began to think she was right about the Sultan. I tried

to move my thoughts from the fear of what would become of us and put them on Shahrazad. I imagined her at the celebration. I pictured the Sultan . . . *cherishing* her. My visions of her appearing at our cell door began to fade.

I fought off the sneaky, disloyal thought that she might have . . . forgotten us.

And so on the seventh day, when I woke from a nap and saw . . . an *apparition* standing at the door, I thought at first that I must be dreaming. This creature was garbed in a dazzling robe of scarlet brocade embroidered with gold, and shrouded in a gauzy silky veil. In the light that slanted in through the high window, I could see that her hands were dyed with intricate henna patterns, like a bride.

"Put on your veils," she was saying, "and come with me!"

I stared at her openmouthed, then turned to find Zaynab staring as shamelessly as I.

"Don't sit around gaping, Marjan. *Hurry!*" the apparition said.

And then I knew who she was.

Dunyazad.

"What—" I began.

"We've got to get you out of here. It's all planned. It's not safe for you here anymore, after what happened to Soraya. So—"

"Soraya?" My mind was moving slowly. I had waited so long for this moment that I hardly believed in it anymore. "What happened to Soraya?" I asked.

"Oh— You don't know anything, do you?"

"We heard the crier say that the Sultan was going to celebrate his marriage to Shahrazad. But . . . but *you* . . . all dressed up to marry . . ." A sudden, horrible thought occurred to me. "She's not," I said. "He didn't—"

"My sister's fine," Dunyazad said. "Put on your veils! I'll tell you all about it on the way."

Zaynab and I threw on our veils and followed Dunyazad out the door and into the narrow hallway. At the end of the hall, near the stairs, I saw the storyteller and the eunuch, waiting.

Dunyazad spoke to us as we hurried toward them. "The Sultan is celebrating his marriage to my sister, as you heard. He begged her forgiveness and said he'll never stop blaming himself for the past as long as he lives. He promised to honor her above all other women, and she doesn't have to tell stories anymore unless she wants to. And . . ." She paused. "And his brother is marrying me."

I stopped, stared. The Sultan's brother . . . who had been killing his wives every night, too . . . Dunyazad was going to *marry* him?

"Come *along*, Marjan!" Dunyazad took my hand, pulled me beside her. The storyteller and the eunuch started up the stairs; Dunyazad followed, with me and Zaynab close behind.

"Soraya was found drowned in the baths," Dunyazad said. "The Khatun says it must have been an accident, but everyone else thinks the Khatun had someone kill her. That's why Shahrazad didn't want you released from the dungeon. To protect you from . . . *accidents*, until we could get you safely away."

Soraya . . . drowned? It hit me in the pit of my stomach. And . . . *away*. Where was *away*? I couldn't take in everything she had told me. There was too much of it. It had come too fast.

When we came out at the top of the stairs, Dunyazad led us down a deserted hallway. The music and voices swelled louder.

"The Sultan has invited all his subjects—high and low—to partake in the feasting, as a sign of reconciliation between him and them," Dunyazad went on. "For the grief he's caused them. For their daughters. And to celebrate his vow never to do what he did again. People are arriving from all parts of the kingdom."

"So . . . *you* are getting married today?" I asked.

Dunyazad nodded. "It's a celebration for Shahrazad and the Sultan, and the formal marriage for his brother and me."

"But . . . how did you get away? You're the bride. They'll miss you."

Dunyazad grinned, dimpling. "I slipped away. You know I can do that. But I have to be back soon."

Now we turned into a hallway filled with people—women and eunuchs carrying roasted meats and viands and sweetmeats this way and that. I hesitated. "But they'll see us."

"It's all right," Dunyazad said, moving into the hallway. The women hastily veiled themselves when they caught sight of the storyteller. I half expected someone to stop us. But instead, they made way for us. For Dunyazad. Then they knelt, kissed the ground at her feet. She was a queen now. Or would be very soon. We picked our way among the prostrate bodies, moving toward the kitchen.

"It's all arranged," Dunyazad was saying. "Shahrazad and I planned it, and the Sultan and his brother agreed. Still," she added in a whisper, "we have to get you out quickly, because the Khatun could make trouble."

"*What's* arranged?" I asked. "Where are we going?"

Dunyazad stopped at the outer kitchen door, gave each of us a small, heavy brocade bag. "These are gifts from my sister and me. Though we can never repay all of you for what you've done. There's a caravan outside. The driver will take you to my husband's old palace in Samarkand. The Sultan has made my father viceroy there—he will be in command. He'll need a reliable vizier," she said, nodding at the storyteller. She turned to the eunuch. "And a head eunuch for the harem." She smiled at Zaynab. "And a governor of messenger pigeons. And, Marjan," she added, "I'm thinking Zaynab will need a helper. Someone to learn the art, take over for her when she's too old. And they'll also need a good story-teller in the harem. Now, go! The caravan's just outside the door. Everyone's waiting."

The storyteller, the eunuch, and Zaynab slipped out the door, but I didn't move. "Would you do something for me?" I asked. "Send someone to give this to Uncle Eli where I lived before I came here? And tell him . . . tell him to tell Auntie Chava . . . what's become of me?"

Dunyazad nodded, but pushed away the brocade bag when I held it out to her. "Keep it, Marjan. Shahrazad put some of her own most precious treasures in there for you. Your friends will be provided for—you have my word. They'll have the protection of the queen. Now, *go!*"

I still didn't move. "But, Dunyazad, how will you . . . The Sultan's brother, he's been killing his wives, too. How . . ." I didn't know how to say it. *How will you make sure he doesn't kill you? And even if he never does, how will you ever love him?*

"He says he's changed now," Dunyazad said. "He's

vowed to honor me above all other women and never to hurt me. He is . . . gentle with me," she said. "And *very* pleasing to look upon." She smiled bravely, but I saw a tremor in it. "Anyway," she said, "he's moving here to govern side by side with his brother. Shahrazad requested it, so that *we* would not be parted, and the two brothers agreed." She hesitated, and her eyes grew serious. "It's the best we could hope for, Marjan. I can live this way."

She clasped me to her, then held me at arm's length. "I've already been gone too long. May Allah give you a long and happy life. I'll never forget you."

Then she nudged me out the door.

Heat and blinding sunlight engulfed me in a wave. Revelers crowded the street. Above the clamor of voices rose the music of horns and drums and tambourines. Lengths of colorful cloth hung down from the roofs of buildings and canopied the streets. A man passed by me swinging a censer; the fragrance of incense mingled with the smells of animals and sweat and dung. Above the crowd, I could see camels' humped backs. I moved toward them and saw Zaynab sitting in a pannier basket slung over the side of a kneeling camel. A pigeon perched on her shoulder, pecking at her hair. She waved and called out, "Hurry, my dear!" I pushed through the crowd; a man standing by the camel helped me into the pannier, which had a canopy and a cushioned seat. The man moved to the front of the camel and pulled on its lead rope; I held on tight as the camel lurched to its feet, pitching us forward and backward and forward again as its legs slowly unfolded. Now we were high up in the air. Traveling like Princess Budur. From up there I could see the whole caravan of camels and riders. I spotted Shahrazad and

Dunyazad's father, and the scar-faced man who had frightened me at the storyteller's home. The eunuch mounted up on a camel, and the storyteller, astride another one, turned back and waved at us. His glance snagged on Zaynab's; she blushed and turned away. He *does* like her, I thought.

But where was Ayaz? I wondered. Surely the storyteller wouldn't leave without him!

The camels plodded forward with a rolling gait, their bells jingling, their tassels swaying. We moved against the current of celebrating people, who flowed through the street toward the palace: on foot, in carts, in litters; camelback, horseback, donkeyback, muleback.

It was odd how, in the middle of this joyous celebration—Shahrazad's triumph!—I felt so sad. Things were ending: my life in the city, any hope of ever seeing Auntie Chava and Uncle Eli again. Or Shahrazad and Dunyazad. Or little Mitra. Or . . .

I had a sudden vision of Soraya floating facedown in a beautiful pond, and my sadness deepened. I had never thought of her as a friend, even though she had helped me. But she had only been trying to survive—like the rest of us. She had made her choice and had died for it.

I turned to look back and watched the palace shrink behind us, thinking again of Shahrazad, married to a man whose deeds were so steeped in blood that he would never shed the guilt of them. I could feel sorry for him now—could understand his crippled heart—but I didn't think I could forgive him, as Shahrazad had done. I wasn't sure that it was *right* to forgive him.

And Dunyazad . . . I would pray for her. *She* would not forgive easily.

All at once, above the flutes and tambourines and glad

voices, I heard a shout: "Uncle!" I twisted round and searched through the crowd until I saw someone running toward us. It was Ayaz.

The storyteller called out to him, and then Ayaz was running past us, scrambling up behind the storyteller onto his camel. Ayaz said something to the storyteller; their camel wheeled round and drew up beside us. "Marjan!" Ayaz said, smiling wide. "You owe me money. Lots of it!"

I nodded, feeling an answering smile steal across my face.

"Where are we going?" Ayaz asked the storyteller.

"To a new life!" the storyteller shouted.

A new life. Like in stories, where you could set off on an adventure and come to a land where having a crippled foot or being born poor or a woman was no obstacle to living out your dreams.

I turned forward, tried to catch a glimpse of the green hills beyond the city, imagining my new life.

Author's Note

The story of Shahrazad, the queen who saved her own life and the lives of many other women by telling tales for 1001 nights, originated long ago—probably a thousand years or more. Though some scholars have speculated that the story may have begun in India before migrating to Persia, many point to a lost Persian book of fairy tales called *Hazar Afsaneh*, or "Thousand Stories," as the true source. From Persia, Shahrazad's story moved to the Arabic world, where it was performed and passed on, constantly changing, for century after century.

The tales that Shahrazad told come to us from many times and places, including ancient Mesopotamia and India, early medieval Persia and Iraq, and Egypt of the late Middle Ages. Shahrazad and her stories were introduced in the West in 1704 by Antoine Galland. They have continued to be told and retold, becoming beloved of people all over the world.

In writing this novel, I have used Richard F. Burton's English translation—*The Book of the Thousand Nights and a Night*—as my guide. I've added new characters and behind-the-scenes events but have tried not to alter the basic action set out in Burton's version. Since the names in the tale of Shahrazad are of Persian derivation, I have given my story a Persian inflection. Where I have made up characters not included in the original tale, I have given most of them Persian names. Shahrazad, Dunyazad, and their father, as well as Shahryar and his brother, are introduced in the original tale. Marjan, Ayaz, Mitra, the bazaar storyteller, and most other characters are my own inventions. Zaynab was inspired by one of the stories Shahrazad told, "The Wily Dalilah and Her Daughter Zaynab."

In my novel, women are veiled in the Persian way, with an older version of the *chador*. While veils in many Arabic countries cover most or all of the face, the Persian veil covers hair, ears, and neck, but leaves the "moon of the face" exposed. I have also followed the Islamic practice of combining some of the traditional prayer sessions, so there are three instead of five every day. One thing that might confuse Western readers is the practice of "making ablutions touching earth." In Islam, it is important to wash in a certain way before praying. However, if water is not available, it is permissible to make ablutions with sand or earth.

The tale of Julnar is part of what Burton calls the nucleus—thirteen tales common to early manuscripts of Shahrazad's stories. The order of the tales varies in different versions; I have taken the liberty of setting the Julnar tale last.

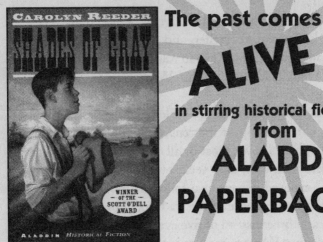

The past comes ALIVE

in stirring historical fiction **from**

ALADDIN PAPERBACKS

☐ **The Best Bad Thing**
Yoshiko Uchida
0-689-71745-8

☐ **Fever 1793**
Laurie Halse Anderson
0-689-83858-1

☐ **The Journey Home**
Yoshiko Uchida
0-689-71641-9

☐ **Shades of Gray**
Carolyn Reeder
0-689-82696-6

☐ **Brothers of the Heart**
Joan W. Blos
0-689-71724-5

☐ **Forty Acres and Maybe a Mule**
Harriette Gillem Robinet
0-689-83317-2

☐ **The Journey to America Saga**
Sonia Levitin
Annie's Promise
0-689-80440-7
Journey to America
0-689-71130-1
Silver Days
0-689-71570-6

☐ **Steal Away Home**
Lois Ruby
0-689-82435-1

☐ **Caddie Woodlawn**
Carol Ryrie Brink
0-689-71370-3

☐ **A Gathering of Days**
Joan W. Blos
0-689-71419-X

☐ **Under the Shadow of Wings**
Sara Harrell Banks
0-689-82436-X

☐ **The Eternal Spring of Mr. Ito**
Sheila Garrigue
0-689-71809-8

☐ **A Jar of Dreams**
Yoshiko Uchida
0-689-71672-9

☐ **The Second Mrs. Giaconda**
E. L. Konigsburg
0-689-82121-2

Aladdin Paperbacks • Simon & Schuster Children's Publishing • www.SimonSaysKids.com